UNICORN

Addiction, Guilt and a Decision That Will Change Her Life

by

L.E. Get

TELEMACHUS PRESS

Cover designed by Kristin Bryant/Kristin Designs

Cover art:
Copyright © Dollar Photo Club/54618182/two women rear view
Copyright © Dollar Photo Club/20487746/RARE EARTH
Copyright © Dollar Photo Club/59750578/Denver City Park

Published by Telemachus Press, LLC
http://www.telemachuspress.com

Visit the author website:
http://www.authorleget.wordpress.com

Library of Congress Control Number: 2015943456

ISBN: 978-1-941536-95-7 (eBook)
ISBN: 978-1-941536-96-4 (Paperback)

Version 2015.06.08

10 9 8 7 6 5 4 3 2 1

UNICORN

Addiction, Guilt and a Decision That Will Change Her Life

Chapter 1

I'M INVISIBLE TO most people, unless I have something to give them. Saying no feels like I'm pushing away the people I want to be close to. So when my mother called to tell me she needed me to come home because my sister, Amelia, was sick and in the hospital again, I grudgingly boarded a plane back to Denver to deal with my family.

Exhausted and needing a distraction, I was hoping I could sleep away my anger and resentment on the long flight home from Dubai. I reclined my seat, closed my eyes and imagined the celebration of the successful show and after-party I was missing. While I was packing my bags and trying to book a flight, the other models were mingling with the hot, new UAE designers looking to sign models. The show had been a highlight in my career, a game-changing event that could have secured a generous contract. Instead, I was sitting next to a woman wearing too much rose-scented perfume, on a long flight home to participate in Amelia's drama. I reached up, twisted on the air and closed my eyes once more replaying my mother's phone call.

~~~~

"Scarlet, can you come home right away? How long will it take you to get home? Amelia's in the hospital," Mom said.

So Amelia is in the hospital again, for the umpteenth time. What else is new? "I'm not supposed to leave until tomorrow, maybe the next day. We just finished the show and I still need to wrap things up."

"Your sister needs you here right away. She's very sick… I need you here." She started to cry.

I took a deep breath, then spoke without thinking. "Amelia needs detox and treatment… She's probably out of prescription drugs and needs a refill," I added callously.

~~~~

I hated feeling so heartless, and tears escaped from my closed eyes. I was frustrated and tired. I needed sleep. I would have a lot to deal with once I was home.

Chapter 2

THANKS TO SOME delays, Dubai to Denver had been my longest trip, a little over thirty hours. I left Dubai just after midnight, and after making my connection, I was finally back in Denver. It was late and eerily dark and quiet at the airport. I stepped off the curb and into the Town Car while the driver lifted my bags into the open trunk. I was jetlagged but decided to have him drive me to the hospital, even though I was not sure Amelia could have visitors this late. But I was home, and I wanted to see her.

As I walked the hall of the surprisingly empty hospital searching for Amelia's room, the contrast between this place and where I had been just hours before brought me back to earth. Here, I was not a super model living a glamorous life. Here, I was wearing sweats, my hair was in a ponytail and I wore no makeup. Here, I was not desperately trying to secure connections with designers or get the attention of the handsome music coordinator I secretly prayed liked me too. Here, I felt much more alone. Here, I was just Scarlet, Amelia's little sister, in a dysfunctional family.

Amelia was sleeping, so I stood in the doorway and watched her. I hated hospitals and seeing Amelia like this. I nervously rubbed my wrist, feeling the bracelet she had made me a couple years earlier. Making jewelry had been another of her attempts at getting her life on track. I had funded her startup and sold pieces to other models, assistants, and everybody who complimented me on the bracelet. I took it off only when I had to for a shoot.

I raised my arm as if checking the time and looked closely at the bracelet. Amelia had so many wasted talents. Rubbing my fingers against the cool, earthy stones and warm, brown leather, I remembered the day Amelia started her bracelet business.

She had broken up with her boyfriend, then ended up in the hospital with severe back pain. I got back into town for the aftermath. Expecting to see her on the couch or in bed depressed, drunk, or passed out from painkillers, I came home to a very different Amelia—an Amelia I've been searching for ever since.

~~~~

I walked into my townhouse with my suitcase and was greeted with the smell of home cooking. Amelia was in the kitchen, wearing an apron. "Hey Scar! You hungry? I made a roast."

"Starved." Suspiciously, I pulled my suitcase to the hall, dropped my purse, and kicked off my shoes. I stepped into the kitchen and gave her a hug. "How are you doing? How's your back?"

"I'm better than ever." She smiled, then reached for another hug. "I haven't felt this alive for a long time. The sky is bluer, the grass is greener, and I've never felt happier."

"Why, Amelia, what happened? What's going on?" I pulled up a bar stool and watched her take some freshly baked chocolate-chip cookies out of the oven. Amelia looked great, a little heavier, but it suited her nicely. She looked healthy and happy.

"I've decided I don't want a man in my life, at least for a while. They've been nothing but trouble for me. They make me feel bad about being me. I just want to be me and free, without the stress and pressure of a relationship. When I'm with somebody, I start to care only about the man and I stop caring about me. I lose myself. I don't want to do that anymore."

I sat there, stunned. I had never heard or seen Amelia so content and clear minded. And I believed her for the first time in a long time. There was something very different about her.

"Scar, I hate to ask, but I could really use your help with something."

Oh, great, here it comes.

"Well, you know how much I love jewelry—well, bracelets?"

"Yes," I said, raising my eyebrows.

"Well, I want to design bracelets. Make bracelets and sell them."

"I'm in! What do you need?" I said with a huge smile. I always said yes to Amelia before I had the chance to think things through. I was brain-dead around her, it seemed, but always with a gnawing feeling deep in my gut telling me to be careful or I'd get hurt again. I ignored that internal warning when it came to Amelia.

"Okay!" she said and smiled, too, as she pulled the table-cloth back to reveal her workstation of beads, leather straps, stones, tools and already-designed bracelets.

Picking up a few bracelets from the table, I exclaimed, "I love them all. They are beautiful! Beautiful! I want one. Can I buy one? How much are you selling them for?"

"Well, what do you think I should sell them for?"

"How much do they cost to make?"

"...and I have another favor." She took my hand and started to put a bracelet on my wrist. "Being's you're a model, would you be willing to wear it all the time? Maybe even promote it to your supermodel friends?" she said, looking up at me with pleading eyes.

"Of course, Amelia, you don't even have to ask. Put one on Mom, too. She'll sell the crap out of these." I giggled, knowing how proud Mom would be of Amelia and how proud I was of her. "Amelia," I said, looking at the bracelet, "I think you've found your calling."

"Me, too," she said as she pulled a few more from a box. "I made these, too."

I looked through them. "Let's make a plan! Do you have a business name? Or bracelet name?"

"I don't want to get a head of myself. I just like making them, and if I could make a few bucks, I'll be happy."

"Okay, you're right. Let's see how they sell and then we'll…"

"Slow down, Scarlet. Jesus! I just made a few bracelets. I don't even know if this is right for me!"

I'd been through this with Amelia before. She could be off and on as quickly as a light switch. Best not to put pressure on her. I'd made that mistake before. "You're right. I'm sorry, you're right." I giggled, trying to lighten the mood. "I had you opening stores in Miami, New York, and LA." I started laughing. "Let's call Mom and let her pick one. I'm here for you. Whatever you want. You know that, right?"

"Thanks, Scar." She relaxed and started eagerly looking though her beads.

I wanted Amelia to jump on this. I wanted her to lock in and make jewelry her future. I thought this might be the right path to help her overcome her other troubles. Amelia was smart, creative, and talented, and I saw designing bracelets as a perfect fit. Not to mention her beauty alone could sell the bracelets. I could sell them, too, to my many connections, and help create a wonderful success for Amelia. I knew I had to tread lightly, but I was going to try to move this forward for her.

~~~~

As I watched her sleeping in the hospital bed, I noticed she looked a little puffy, her face swollen. Shaking my head in disbelief, I was mad and sad that Amelia couldn't get her life straight even with talent and opportunities. I touched my bracelet one more time, knowing the sadness—and hope—it represented. The day she put that bracelet on my wrist, I made a private commitment to myself that I would not take it off until Amelia was clean and sober.

I kissed my fingertips, blew the kiss toward my beautiful sleeping sister and left the hospital.

Chapter 3

WHEN I GOT home and was alone, the bad memories flooded over me; it happened every time Amelia was in the hospital. I thought back to the missed opportunities when I could have—should have—helped her.

About two months after Amelia started her bracelet business, I came home from one of my favorite shoots, a shoot in Kenya with wild animals in the background. I couldn't wait to tell Amelia all about it, and about wanting to take her and Mom on a safari. I had also picked up some beads I thought Amelia would like, hoping that would get her excited about her bracelets again.

I was off work for two weeks, fingers crossed, and couldn't wait to get back to Amelia and spend time with her. We had plans to go shopping and to the latest movies, to check out new restaurants and to see *The Lion King* at The Buell Theatre. It would be a much-needed break for me, and I thought maybe I could help Amelia get back on track with some good choices for her future. I thought I would help her get back to making jewelry.

When I got home I rushed into my apartment expecting an enthusiastic greeting, but Amelia wasn't home. I hollered, "Amelia," then turned on the lights and opened the blinds, noticing the place was a mess, as usual. "Amelia!" I went into the kitchen and saw an empty vodka bottle on the counter and another one in the garbage can. "Fuck! Amelia!" I panicked and raced down the hall to her room. She wasn't there, but the stench of vomit and stale booze was suffocating. I slammed the door, then looked in the bathroom as I passed. Empty. I felt the ever-present dread that I might find her dead.

I opened my bedroom door and there she was, out cold in my bed and snoring. "Amelia," I said, shaking her leg. "What's going on? Are you sick?"

"Leave me alone," she said. "Get out of here."

"You get out of here! You're in my room!"

"Leave me alone."

"Get your ass out of my bed!" I was furious, my concern turning to rage. I grabbed her leg and yanked her toward the foot of the bed.

"You're such a bitch. I'm sick!" she moaned.

"You're loaded, not sick! I come home hoping for some R n' R and instead my room's a mess, the place is a mess, my sister's a mess, and I'm the one who has to clean it all up. Get your ass out of my bed!" I reached for her leg and pulled her again, but her other foot shot back at me, landing right in my chest with a hard thud. I fell flat on my back on my bedroom floor, gasping for air and afraid she had broken my ribs. I was frantic as I tried to catch my breath, thinking she might come to my aid. But she didn't care that she had kicked me so hard she knocked the wind out of me. She just scooted back toward the top of the bed and pulled the covers over her.

Once the shock wore off and my breathing had returned to normal, I left my room, slammed the door, and rushed back to the kitchen. I picked up the phone and dialed 911.

"911. What is your emergency?"

When I heard those words, *what is your emergency?* I started to cry. "I'm not sure I'm calling the right number, but I need the police to come to my house. My address is…"

"What's the problem?"

"My sister is drunk. I think she's hurting herself and she needs to go to detox."

"Okay, honey, we have a patrol car in the area. They're on the way. Do you need an ambulance?"

"I don't know. I don't think so."

After I hung up, I called Mom who lived only a few blocks away. "Mom, I called the police on Amelia. Will you come over?"

"I'll be right there," she said. Within minutes, there was a knock on the door, and I let the two officers in. Mom was right behind them.

After my quick explanation of what had happened, the female officer asked, "Where is your sister? We'd like to talk to her."

"She's in the back bedroom." I said, and watched them walk down the hall. Then I turned to Mom and said, "Amelia's really drunk and it's ten in the morning. She's sick, Mom. She needs help. I want the police to take her to detox. Will you support me on this?"

"Yes, whatever you think is right. I haven't talked to her for a week. She's mad at me again."

The officers stepped into the living room and said, "The door's locked. We tried to get her to open the door but... nothing."

I went into the kitchen and found a pen. Pulling the ink tube out with my teeth, I walked back to the bedroom door, slid the pen part into the door knob hole until it clicked, then walked in. "Amelia the police are here to take you to detox. You're sick and you need help. We're going to get you some help."

"Get out of my room!"

"This is my room," I quietly said to the male officer. "She doesn't even know she's in my room."

"Why don't you let us have a little time with her?"

Mom and I went back into the living room. "Why is she mad at you this time?" I asked.

"Who knows for sure." We sat in silence. My heart was racing. I was breathing hard and I was scared. Then Mom said, "Your place is a mess... smells."

Duh! I held back my anger and didn't say anything.

"This is awful. Has she been throwing up or something?"

I stared at her, unbelieving. *Are you fucking kidding me right now?* I wanted to explode and release all of my frustration by yelling at her, but I held it in because I knew it wouldn't help the situation. I took a deep breath, then said, "Mom, I just worry about her all the time. I'm so afraid she's killing herself.

Every time I come home from a shoot, I'm afraid I'm going to find her dead. I'm afraid she's going to mix the wrong pill with the wrong drink. I'm afraid she's going to forget she took something for her back pain, then take more and she's going to OD." I started to break down. "Every time you call me, I'm scared. I think you're going to tell me that my sister's dead. Every time my phone rings, I'm afraid it's bad news, very bad news, about Amelia. I hate living like this."

Mom started to cry. It seemed she had similar fears.

"That's why we need to get her help. I'm here for two weeks. We can get a lot of help for her in two weeks. And I'll come back and help when I'm done with my next job."

The male officer came down the hall. "Well, she sobered up quickly when she saw us. She seems okay. She said she has plans to move with her boyfriend to New Mexico. And, yes, she had a little too much to drink. She said they had a fight last night and she drank a lot, then this morning tried to drink to get rid of the hangover. It didn't work."

"She doesn't have a boyfriend," I said.

Mom interrupted, "Well, there's some guy she's spending time with."

"Who?"

"I don't know. I think he's from New Mexico," Mom said.

"After talking to Amelia, she doesn't seem to be suicidal, which is what we look for. We want to know that she isn't going to hurt herself or others," the officer said. "And because she has plans for her future, well, that's a sign that she has no plans to take her own life. But she is very intoxicated. We can take her in, but the problem is, they can't force her to stay and they could release her at three in the morning. It's hard to say when she would be free to go, but they'll let her go. She doesn't want to go to detox, but this is your place. She's obviously destructive, and we certainly can take her in."

I looked at Mom. "Would she call you to come and get her? Because I know she wouldn't call me."

"I don't think she'd call me either. Probably her new boyfriend," Mom said.

"Is he a drunk?"

Mom looked at me like, 'Come on, you have to ask?'

I looked at the cop and took a deep breath. "What would you do?"

"If I were you, I'd start going to Al-Anon. She has to want to stop drinking. You can't force her. And right now, you two are the ones suffering, not her. She has no idea the pain she's putting you through."

"But what if taking her in gets her moving in the right direction?"

"It won't, unless she's ready. And at this point, there will not be counseling, strictly detox, which is a horrible process for somebody who has been drinking every day, like you said your sister has."

"She's moving to New Mexico, huh?" I said.

"That's what she said."

"I just can't deal with her anymore. She's destroying me and she's killing my mom." I started crying again.

"Al-Anon," he said.

Amelia came walking down the hall toward us. She was wearing black thong panties and a grey half-shirt barely covering her chest. As hard as she tried to prove to all of us that she was fine, with each step she took, she fell into the wall on either side of the hallway—the wall was the only thing keeping her on her feet. She made her way to the couch and said, "Bitch" to me as she passed. She plopped down and covered herself up with a throw blanket. The female officer looked at me sadly, sympathizing with my predicament.

Amelia said, "Scarlet, I'm not going to detox! I had too much to drink, that's it. I'm calling my boyfriend, and he's coming to get me. I'm moving out!"

Those words broke my heart. I had just pushed her further away from me when all I wanted was to be close to her. "Why not get some help right now, Amelia? I will find you the best treatment, in the best facility. I will do anything to help you. I don't care how much it costs…"

"Oh, big model doesn't care how much it costs. Why don't you straighten out your own fuckin' life?"

The jabs never stop hurting, even when I knew she was drunk and she wasn't herself. "Amelia, if I didn't have money, I'd still get you the right help. I'd take out a loan. Why won't you let me help you?"

"Why won't you leave me alone? Why can't you two just leave me alone?" She looked at the female officer and said, "I'm not going!"

"It's up to you," the officer said to me.

I stood there frozen, unable to make a decision. "What would happen to her in detox? How can I know for sure she's safe?" I envisioned her helpless and being in a jail cell or getting raped or beaten up by somebody. I didn't really know what detox was.

Before they could answer my questions, I said, "I guess I can't make her want to get better. She's moving out. Maybe I'll try that Al-Anon." I escorted the police officers to the door and thanked them again.

~~~~

Another missed opportunity to help Amelia.

It seemed that fear kept me from helping my sister, but what was I so afraid of? I just didn't know. Every time I tried to support her, somehow I failed.

Pulling my suitcase toward my bedroom, I felt like the wind had been kicked out of me again as I passed my sister's very clean, very organized and very abandoned bedroom.

Chapter 4

MY NIGHT WAS restless. I was still adjusting to the time difference from my recent travels and being in my own bed, but the worst part was worrying about what was happening with Amelia. At three in the morning I got up, started the coffee maker, and took a long, hot shower. Wrapped in my favorite white robe, I sat on the couch in my living room and stared into the dark morning as I sipped hot coffee.

My place was so clean and boring. No life between these walls. Its predictability was comforting, but also disturbing. My place matched my life—nothing stood out, nothing was interesting. It was all very forgettable, just like me.

In contrast, I thought about the many times Amelia lived with me and how my home took on a whole new ambience—chaos, drama, excitement, and although most of it was negative, it was still excitement. I chuckled at one of the most humiliating episodes Amelia had put me through.

~~~~

I had hit a low in my career, and I was heartbroken over a man. Amelia had just broken up with her latest boyfriend, so we had been talking on the phone more often. She was anxious for me to get home. I was also looking forward to some sister-time full of sappy movies, ice cream, good talks, and maybe some tears over men.

I had met a guy on set about a month before, and I kept running into him. We had been making small talk, and I had the feeling that he was interested in me. I was so excited that I made the mistake of telling one of my friends, another model, that I liked him. The next day, she was hanging all over him. And just like that, he was no longer interested in me, probably never really was anyway, but I'd had a little hope. By the time I was headed back to Denver, I was pretty sure they were in love and would probably live happily ever after. I was depressed.

When I got home, my depression quickly disappeared as I went into survival mode. Amelia had moved back in with her boyfriend without letting me know, and had left my place trashed. An odd odor inside made me afraid that there was a gas leak, so I went back out to my car, where I had left my luggage, purse, and cell phone and called the fire department. I was humiliated and embarrassed as the firefighters in full gear walked through my townhouse. It was such a mess—dirty dishes everywhere, dirty clothes all over, and food lying around turning moldy. I sat in my car and waited as they searched my home for the gas leak. The head guy walked up to my car in his yellow firefighter suit and said they couldn't find a gas leak; they, too, smelled the pungent odor, but it wasn't gas. They didn't know what it was, so they set up big fans to try to air it out before they left.

Once I was back inside, I searched for the source of the smell. While cleaning and sniffing around like a dog, I found a clothesbasket on my dryer. I lifted some of the dirty clothes and almost passed out from the stench coming from the rotten, nasty clothes with something spilled on them. I threw the clothes and clothes basket outside by my garage then dialed Amelia's number.

"You stupid bitch! Do you have any idea the shit you put me through? I've had it. You left my place in such a mess that I had to call the fire department. You stupid fucking bitch! You better get your life straightened out! I'm so sick of your shit. You are no longer allowed here. I'm changing the locks. I'm throwing all your nasty, smelly shit out, so if you want your stuff, it will be in the driveway. I'm all done with you!" I hung up on her before she could say a word, then realizing that she had probably hung up within the first second, when I called her a stupid bitch.

I ran around my place and picked up everything of Amelia's that stank, including old pizza boxes lying around and empty booze bottles, and I piled them onto the clothesbasket in the driveway. Everything else I found of hers that didn't smell, I threw into her room. I called her back and left a message. "I don't know how you can continue to treat me and my place with such disrespect, but I need you to come over and get your stuff out of here. Some of your things are in the driveway and some in your room. You're not coming back here so you better play nice with your boyfriend."

~~~~

The memory still stung, as I took another sip of my cooling coffee and another look around my clean home. I preferred the order but still missed Amelia. I wondered what happened to her to make her life such a mess. What caused her to care so little about people around her? This puzzle gnawed at me almost daily. I got up to get another cup of coffee.

~~~~

Amelia had been an alcoholic and drug addict since high school. I blamed the dick she dated while she was still a sophomore. He was a senior who smoked cigarettes across the street before class and was thought to be a drug dealer. His parents were the hippie, biker type, and although I didn't have proof, I'm sure he was the one who supplied the drugs and alcohol to Amelia during that impressionable time. He dumped her just before he dropped out of school, leaving her heartbroken with a need to party.

Or it could have been Amelia's high school best friend, Coco, who got her hooked. Rumor had it that she got the nickname Coco because of her love for cocaine. She wanted to be a model, so she started taking drugs, cocaine mainly, sometimes speed, so she could stay thin. Coco did a few local modeling gigs, like wearing wedding and bridesmaid dresses at the mall and being a sexy hostess at a car auction, but because Coco fell in love with a religious college boy just before graduation, she ended her drug use, gave up her modeling dreams and her friendship with my sister and settled on becoming an extremely religious wife and mother.

Although hurt from that loss, Amelia never lacked for friends, especially the male type, and she easily ran off with other drinking and drugging friends. There was never a shortage of that type of friend because misery loves company. I didn't know how or why Amelia started down the path of destruction; the whole thing never made sense to me because I knew that Amelia was better than that.

After Amelia lost her friendship with Coco, I remember hoping that we would become closer, maybe best friends. But that didn't happen. We'd never been close, but I'd always secretly hoped we would be better friends. I had tried so hard to make her want to spend time with me. I was always there for her, trying to help every time her heart was broken or she lost a friend. Maybe I loved her too much, so it was easy for her to walk on me—I allowed it. I was pretty sure I loved her more than she had ever loved me.

I tried to remember when Amelia came through for me, when she put her life aside to be there for me. I gulped down my now-cool second cup of coffee, still needing the solace of caffeine. I remembered a time I thought she was there for me, when I didn't feel a lot of support from Mom or my best friend, Tabitha. It seemed Amelia was my greatest support, but then I realized, like every other time, I was really the one who was there for her.

Amelia used to join me in New York and Miami and at other shoots and events. I think she secretly loved that Coco was never a model but her little sister was, and not just a small-time model but a model who was making great money doing runways and spreads in magazines. I didn't care why Amelia wanted to spend time with me, I was just happy to spend time with her.

But then during one of the after-parties, I looked across the room at Amelia and saw she was completely wasted, almost to the point of unconsciousness. A man sitting next to her was rubbing her breast and had his hand down his pants, touching himself. I rushed over, helped her up, and we went back to my room in the hotel. It wasn't the first time I'd seen men use her, but it was the first time it was so blatantly in my face.

The next morning she didn't remember anything, and I realized that by inviting her to be with me during shows, I was supplying her with drugs, alcohol, and sometimes, seedy men. Amelia wasn't there to support me or be a part of my life; she was there for the parties and the escape from reality.

~~~~

A few years ago, Amelia also started suffering from lower back pain, which gave her access to prescription pain medications. From then on, her back became the excuse for everything bad in her life. It also gave her a reason to stay on the couch in front of the TV and no longer participate in life or try to get her life back on track.

~~~~

Frustrated with thinking about all this, I knew I couldn't pinpoint the source of Amelia's problems. Was it her first boyfriend? Was it Coco? Was it her back? Or did the real problem kick in when she was hanging around me while I was building my career? I took my coffee cup to the kitchen, rinsed it, and put it in the dishwasher. I wanted answers. I needed a reason. If I knew the root cause or the person responsible for Amelia's addiction, maybe then we could find a way to fix it. But what if nobody was to blame except Amelia herself?

Chapter 5

AMELIA WAS STILL sleeping peacefully when I got to the hospital a little after six that morning. I hadn't seen her look so innocent and beautiful for a long time. Seeing her look so lovely reminded me of a time she moved back in with me, adopted a cat, and let me in on her big secret—she was pregnant. I kept her secret.

She always looked peaceful when she was sleeping, but when she was awake her face looked entirely different—tired, angry, scared. She still looked puffy to me, so I wondered if they were giving her too much IV fluid. She moved slightly and I noticed a big bruise on her side. She wasn't looking good.

What happened to you, Amelia? Why did you end up with addictions? Why weren't you strong enough? I know you're strong enough. Why do you continue to waste your life? I'm tired of seeing you like this. Why aren't you tired of living like this?

I wanted to rescue her. I wanted to unhook her IV, pick her up, and carry her out of there. I wanted to fix her. Why couldn't I save her? I quietly pulled a chair over and sat next to her. At that angle I could see the bruise was bigger than I thought, extending below her lower ribs and over toward her stomach. I gently covered her with the blanket and watched her sleep.

Amelia was blessed with many gifts. She had a great body and was beautiful, so she had her pick of men. I, on the other hand, had always been the shy one. Men seemed to look right through me. I was the awkward, lanky, ugly girl in high school. I wasn't good in school or sports, and I had only one good friend. Tabitha was just as awkward, but she was smart and willing to help me along enough so that I was able to graduate with my class.

Even though I wasn't smart and I was younger, I could see that Amelia was making dumb mistakes, and I couldn't understand how somebody so smart, beautiful, and talented could be so stupid—the endless drinking, drugging, and sleeping around. If I'd had her good fortune, I would have gone to college, found a wonderful career, married the popular, athletic, successful guy and started a small family. I would have lived the dream: two beautiful kids, family vacations, stunning and successful friends. Maybe my husband would get into politics and I would support him in his wish to improve the world, or at least his community. I always thought Amelia would have that life, with kids and a good husband. I could see her as a politician's wife.

Amelia opened her eyes and said, "Hi."

"Hi," I said, pulling the chair closer to the bed before taking her shaking hand. "How are you doing?"

"I think pretty good," she whispered.

I smiled. "What's been happening? Is it your back again?"

"I don't think so. They're running tests… not sure yet."

Amelia's color looked a little off, so in my mind I was prepared for the results to show liver damage. I secretly hoped if she was that sick with serious organ trouble, this would be her bottom, and she'd get her life back—a second chance. Maybe this would be the wakeup call she needed. Because I was pretty sure the liver could repair itself.

"How was Dubai?"

Ugh! Every time I've come running to her, she has a smugness about her, like she was mentally challenging me, telling me, "I know I can make you jump when I say jump." Her asking about Dubai felt like a jab, so I jabbed back. "Great! But I had to leave a day too early, so you should have waited a day to get sick." I smiled and squeezed her hand as if I were joking, but I felt the usual hint of resentment. I was tired of jumping when she said jump. I wanted to be close to her, but she could get under my skin so swiftly.

Mom, who also jumped when Amelia said jump, stepped into the room. "Good morning honey," she said to Amelia. "How are you feeling?"

"Pretty good," she said unconvincingly, to get more sympathy from Mom.

"Can I get you anything?" Mom asked.

"I'd really like some ice water."

"Scarlet, can you go and get her some ice water? By the way, how was your trip home?"

"Great," I said, feeling the resentment growing. I left the room and walked to the nurse's station to ask where I could get some ice water.

The nurse happily showed me the refrigerator full of Ensure and juices and an assortment of teas. She showed me the ice water machine and where to get coffee. "Help yourself. And of course the cafeteria is downstairs if there's anything else you might want," she said, then hurried off.

I filled Amelia's glass and took my time walking back to her room. I still couldn't believe how Mom babied her after everything Amelia had put her through. And even though Mom basically ignored me, I knew it was because Amelia took up all her energy. If Amelia hadn't had all the drama and chaos, Mom would have had time to acknowledge me and my career. Maybe she would have been proud of me. As I walked down the hallway, I saw the cleaning staff stripping the bed in one of the rooms, and an unwanted memory came rushing back.

~~~~

"Scarlet, your sister," which is how most of my conversations started with my mom, "spent the night here with her boyfriend and this morning after they left, I went in to strip the bed and I almost had a heart attack. There was blood everywhere. I mean everywhere. It even soaked into the mattress pad. I know they were drinking, because I found a big empty vodka bottle in their room. She must have had her period and they had sex and made a mess and didn't care enough to tell me, or strip the bed and throw it in the wash for me. Or do you think she is just too crazy to even know what she did?"

"That is disgusting! Are you serious? She really did that?"

"Yes, I'm serious. I know you've said she has no respect for other people, and for the first time, I see your point. How could she be so irresponsible and inconsiderate?"

"I don't think she realizes the mess she leaves, literally, for the rest of us to clean up. Maybe she thinks she is so much better or more important than us that we should clean up after her. It's our duty to make her life easy, and so we do." I paused. "I think you should bag up the sheets and mail them to her. Don't wash them. I'll buy you some new sheets."

"I could never do that."

"Yeah, I know, and that's why she continues to get away with walking all over everybody around her, especially us, the people who love her the most. All her other so-called friends have just dropped out of her live. We stay because we're family."

"Well, maybe her back was bothering her and *he* threw the comforter over the bed and she forgot. I just don't think she would ever do that to me. I mean, isn't she embarrassed?"

"We're talking about Amelia; she doesn't think like normal people. Mom, I have to catch my flight. Love you."

~~~~

With the memory of the bloody sheets still vivid in my mind, I stepped into Amelia's room and handed her the water.

"How far did you have to go to get it?" she asked. That was the funny thing about Amelia. She could say something that felt like a jab, but then easily make it sound like I was too sensitive.

I decided not to play the game. "I'm sorry it took so long," I said, already knowing that she'd say something like, 'No, I meant that I didn't want you to have to go out of your way for me.' It seemed to be a little act for Mom.

"I just didn't want to be too much trouble for you. Thank you for the water," she said.

I was close. "You're welcome." I looked at Mom to see her smiling at how thoughtful her daughter Amelia was to her little sister. "When will you know what's going on with you? If it's just your back or…"

"Oh, *just* my back?" Amelia snapped. "You don't know what I've been through."

"I just mean your back pain isn't life-threatening, right? That's all I meant." I was so frustrated I wanted to leave the room again, but instead I sat down and kept quiet while listening to Mom baby-talk Amelia.

"Honey, do you think you're having more back spasms? Or what do you think is wrong? They don't seem to be in a hurry to discharge you."

"I'm not sure, Mom," Amelia said.

Truthfully, I didn't have a lot of sympathy for Amelia even after her so-called back problems. A few years earlier, I had been on a shoot in Grand Cayman when I ended up in the hospital with back pain. I was scared. Besides hating hospitals and wanting out, what I remembered most was that the Jamaican nurses kept calling me Charlotte, and I was in too much pain to correct them; I just wanted to go home. When they discharged me from the hospital, I noticed the prescription they gave me for Percocet, was made out to Charlotte. I never filled the prescription; I never needed to.

After that experience, I was afraid my health was failing and I might end up like Amelia, with chronic back pain, so I researched causes of back problems. I learned that my problem was mainly because of dehydration. I had been on the beach in the hot sun that day. I had also spent several hours on a bumpy boat ride in the salty air and sun. I didn't drink enough water, so I was dehydrated, and I ended up in the hospital with a back ache. Once home, I went to physical therapy and learned what I needed to do to take care of myself. I drank more water, exercised to strengthen my back, and moved on with my life.

With Amelia drinking so much dehydrating alcohol, it seemed obvious that she was constantly dehydrated and not taking care of herself. Her back pain seemed to be more of an excuse she could use whenever she wanted to be left alone or babied. It also gave her a reason to keep drinking and taking pills.

It just seemed that Amelia didn't want to get better. I thought that if she would stop drinking and stay healthy, her life would improve. But I didn't see her doing anything to fix her situation, not even going to physical therapy for her back. Amelia liked the attention and the access to pain meds more than she wanted a happy, healthy life for herself. Rehashing this in my mind made me wonder if the back pain led to her addiction.

~~~~

"I'll be okay, Mom," I heard Amelia say, bringing me back to the hospital room.

I realized that Mom was crying, so I said, "We know, we just want better for you." I had meant to say that we worried about her, but it came out wrong and she jumped on it.

"Did you hear that, Mom?" she said, pointing her shaky hand at me. "She acts like this is a choice for me, that I like being in the hospital." She looked at me. "You're sick, Scarlet. You're sick in your head."

"Oh, honey, Scarlet didn't mean it like that. She just doesn't want to see you in pain anymore. She wants to see you healthy. And so do I. We all want you to have a better life than in and out of hospitals." She caressed Amelia's forehead, then looked at me. "Isn't that what you meant, Scarlet?"

"Of course that's what I meant." I stood up. "I'm sad, Amelia. I worry about you," I said, wondering why everything I said came out wrong to Amelia. I had to get some fresh air. When I stepped outside of the hospital, I could smell cigarette smoke. Another addiction I despised. *Seriously?* I turned and walked back into the hospital and straight to the cafeteria to get some water and something to eat. I wondered about Amelia's lower back trouble and wondered if it was serious. Mom was right, the hospital hadn't said anything about discharging her.

Back trouble had been an issue with Amelia for some time, and while most people avoid hospitals, Amelia rushed to them. Here she was again, in the hospital, hooked up to an IV, probably getting morphine or Percocet. *What else is new?* I'd seen her hooked up for years. She could always get prescriptions refilled when the pharmacists refused. I figured she was just working her addiction and fooling everybody but me, but what if there was more to it than I realized?

I'd taken her to the hospital when she said she was getting a checkup. I'd watched her get out of my car totally healthy, then ten steps away, bends over and start limping. I had no idea what she told them, but she was admitted and hooked up to morphine or whatever. And then they sent her home with a full bottle of pain medication.

I've heard her tell doctors that she had her purse stolen with her pills inside or that she left her purse on the roof of her car and drove away and the prescription bottle was smashed by another car. I've heard her tell the doctors that she dropped the full opened bottle into the toilet accidentally. I've heard her ask Mom to drive to three different pharmacies to try to get a bottle filled. I've had moments of believing her, too. I wanted desperately to believe my big sister.

Even some of her old friends were sick of her. A friend let her babysit her kids and stay at her house while she and her husband were on a romantic weekend getaway. I guess Amelia drank a couple bottles of their booze, but claimed she had only a few glasses of wine. She said she accidentally dropped and knocked over the other two bottles. The twelve-year-old told her mother that Amelia was sick and throwing up the whole time. Amelia told them she was sick because of her back pain. A few days later her friend called to tell me that they were also missing one of their prescription bottles full of Vicodin. They no longer wanted Amelia in their lives, especially around the kids.

After everything she'd put me through and all that I'd witnessed, our relationship started falling apart. I didn't want to hear her BS anymore; I didn't feel sorry for her anymore; I didn't want to be there for her anymore. But I continued to do it for Mom. And here I was again, as always, putting Amelia and Mom's feelings first in my life.

I bought a small dish of peaches and cottage cheese at the cafeteria and started eating, but my thoughts were still consumed by the situation. I wondered why Mom was always sucked into Amelia's drama and why she always believed everything Amelia said. I thought about the years Mom has had to deal with Amelia and her addictions. I thought about all the phone calls when Mom was crying to me about how worried she was about Amelia. I remembered one call when Mom had said, "I talked to Amelia last week. She was crying and wanted to come home, so I sent her money for a plane ticket and now I can't get ahold of her. She won't answer my calls."

I reminded her to send her the plane ticket and to never send money, but she didn't listen. And a couple months ago Amelia told Mom to pick her up at the airport, but Amelia was a no-show. Mom called me, crying, "I don't know what to do. I can't get ahold of her. Did she take a later flight and forget to tell me? Did she change her plans? Why didn't she tell me?" I told Mom to go home and wait. Amelia didn't bother to call Mom for a week, and she never apologized—she probably didn't remember that she told Mom to pick her up at the airport.

Every time Mom had been hurt or used or let down by Amelia, I'd get those phone calls with Mom crying at the other end. There is nothing worse than hearing my mom cry and knowing I can't help her or comfort her. Amelia's the only one who can fix it, but she doesn't even realize how much she's hurting Mom. My heart breaks for my mom, because she doesn't deserve an addict for a daughter. She should be a happy, middle-aged woman enjoying her novels, friends, traveling and her two grown daughters. But instead she's worried sick every day.

In the past, I had called Amelia to tell her to stop hurting Mom, but it didn't do any good. Amelia was unavailable or incoherent or just didn't care. Sometimes she even blamed the entire misunderstanding on Mom, calling her a drama queen. I wanted to call Amelia every time I got off the phone from Mom, but I didn't anymore.

Chapter 6

I DECIDED NOT to go back to Amelia's room, and I left the hospital. I was agitated and tired. The peaches and cottage cheese hadn't been enough, so I drove to a nearby Perkins and ordered eggs and toast. While I waited, I called Tabitha.

~~~~

Tabitha, my best friend, had been my savior throughout my life. She shared her family with me. Having her mom and dad gave me a haven of normalcy and an escape when I was tired of dealing with my mom and Amelia. Tabitha helped me through high school, and she kept me from being so alone in this world. Every step I walked next to her led me to wonderful things in my own life.

When I went with Tabitha to see her dorm at university, I was discovered by a modeling scout, which secured my future path. I was sitting outside on Tabitha's dorm steps crying about not only losing my best friend to college, but also about being afraid of what lay ahead for my future. I had no direction, and I had no idea what I wanted to do or who I wanted to be when I grew up, and I was growing up. Amelia was no help, and Tabitha was moving away, probably not only physically but maybe emotionally, too. She would make new friends, friends as smart as she was, friends who also wanted to be doctors.

I could see that everybody was worried about me. Tabitha's parents and my mom were making plans for me. I would work and take classes at the community college until I discovered my gifts and decided what I wanted to do. Tabitha wanted me to be a nurse, so just before I graduated from high school, I started working at a nursing home. I was pretty sure I didn't want to be a nurse. I just couldn't find my ambition or direction that inspired me.

I felt very lost until Mae approached me. She was young, just a few years older than me, and new to the business. Her mother was a very successful modeling scout and agent, and Mae believed she could be just as successful as her mother. When she saw me on those steps, she said she noticed my unique look. She took a few pictures and thought I had potential.

I never understood the attraction, but she saw something in me that I still don't see in myself. I'm ugly. I have straight, thin, blond hair and my ears stick out even when my hair is down. I can't hide them. I have a small gap between my front teeth, and I'm skinny and awkward with long limbs and a flat chest. The only thing positive I can say about my looks is that I have nice blue eyes and good skin. But lucky for me, I was the look they wanted.

I have always felt awkward in my skin. I'm not traditionally attractive, but somehow my look translates well in photos, and I know how to walk a runway. It doesn't make sense to me how I ended up the model, but when the opportunity arrived, I became a sponge and learned everything I could about modeling. Wanting to be the best, I knew I had to compensate for my many weaknesses. I learned how to walk by buying a camcorder after my first paycheck and taping myself over and over again until I knew I had a great walk. I walked in every type of shoe and heal and stilts and everything I could get my feet into, even if the shoes were too big or too small. I practiced my walk everywhere: the mall, down the stairs, the grocery store aisles and even my mother's treadmill. I learned about catalog and high fashion and editorial. I went to every fashion show I could, even the wedding shows at the mall. I wanted to learn and I wanted to make it in modeling. I loved every minute of my work; I was rewarded with love and compliments, and that filled me up.

Mae says I was her golden ticket. I was her first real client, and she still says I'm by far her best. I never complain. I never argue. I take in what people tell me. And I learn from the people who want to help me. I've only fallen once on the runway, and I was devastated. I was so insecure the day I fell, I was miserable and feared my career was over. Mae was my savior. She comforted me and told me all the great models have fallen on the catwalk. She said she had never seen anybody fall so gracefully, which I knew was a lie, because I could see the terror on everybody's face.

I had so much encouragement from the start and that encouragement made me want to do well. I felt like some freak of nature, ugly, yet photographers, makeup artists, Mae and her mother kept telling me how beautiful I was, how my shots gave them the chills. "The camera loves you, Scarlet." I'd never had people treat me so well or look at me with such admiration. I guess I had found my gift and discovered what I wanted to do—thanks to Mae believing in me when nobody else did, not even me.

It wasn't anybody's ideal direction for me and my future, but everybody was supportive and a little shocked that I had become so successful. Tabitha originally seemed disappointed in my decision to model but was happy that I'd found a direction in my life. At times, though, it seemed she was now the one sitting on the dorm steps crying, feeling left behind, because I traveled so much. But I would never leave her behind. I wanted her with me always, on every trip. Tabitha was only able to make one trip with me to Canada, nothing exotic, but we had a blast together. And it was good for her to get away from school and the whole doctor thing. She was my very best friend for life, and I knew everything I had was because of her. Tabitha was like my good luck charm, *my* golden ticket.

Even when my mom or somebody we knew saw my picture in a magazine, most people around me didn't take it seriously, didn't believe it was me, or simply didn't understand what it was I did or that I could make a living doing it. Tabitha eventually became one of my biggest fans, and she loved to hear about my travels and stories, and I loved sharing. I also loved to hear about Tabitha and how hard she was working in her medical studies. I admired her so much for being smart and working toward an amazing future. We were both taking our careers seriously.

Tabitha was really the only person I had, my only real friend. Every time I called Mom to talk to her about something good or bad happening in my life, she usually had more important news—the latest on Amelia. So my life was rarely discussed and I eventually stopped sharing. Though everybody was busy, Tabitha and I always made time for each other. She was the one person who never made me feel invisible. She never took more than she gave, in fact, I felt that she always gave to me, more than I gave to her. I loved her more than anybody else in my life and was thankful for her every single day.

~~~~

I didn't have plans for the next few hours, so after the good meal, a venting session with Tabitha and learning about her latest boyfriend, I decided to go home and try to get some rest. I knew it could be a mistake, potentially making it impossible to sleep later that night, but I was exhausted and didn't want to get sick, especially considering I had to spend time in the hospital. I didn't want to pick up any viruses because I was run down.

I snuggled with my pillow, wishing I had slept more on the plane. I thought about how most girls took sleeping pills on the long flights, but maybe because of my sister, I had stayed clean from all drugs and drinking. I'd been tempted to drink or take a sleeping pill, but I couldn't, I was too afraid to end up like Amelia. So maybe one good thing had come out of my sister's mess of a life.

Chapter 7

I SLEPT UNTIL ten that night, then decided to check in on Amelia, secretly hoping she'd be sleeping. I liked her more when she was sleeping. I liked the peacefulness of her company and I could envision her as the sister I knew she could be. I wanted to be close to her.

She was sleeping when I arrived, and I hoped in some way she knew I was there. I sat in the chair close to the door and watched from a distance while she slept. She was so pretty. I looked over her face and then her body; her feet and hands were swollen. She twitched a little, then rolled over, baring half of her body and exposing the unicorn tattoo on her hip. I stepped next to her to cover her back up, but first I took a better look at her tattoo. That unicorn tattoo always reminded me of a stuffed unicorn I had when I was a kid.

~~~~

When we were little, Mom took us to California so we could go to Disneyland and Knotts Berry Farm, and she could spend time with some distant relatives. On the way back to Colorado, we spent one night in Las Vegas where Mom let us play some games at Circus Circus, giving each of us a pocketful of tokens to do with whatever we pleased.

When I saw the huge, beautiful, stuffed white unicorns hanging from the ceiling, I made my way through the crowd to find that game. I watched for a while and discovered that the player had to throw a red ring onto the neck of one of the many bottles sitting in the center of the booth. The game was so busy I had a hard time getting the man's attention to ask if I could play. Finally, he handed me a small bucket with twenty red rings, took my tokens, and then rushed off to help others.

The third ring I threw slid right onto one of the bottles—I had won! The lights started dancing and a siren went off. The guy pointed to me as he said, "We have a winner, folks! This little girl made it look easy! Come on over and give it a try." He looked at me and asked, "What would you like? You can have anything you want." Crowds were gathering and pushing their way in to play the game.

"I'd like the white unicorn."

"You got it!" He gave it a yank and there he stood holding this beautiful, magical unicorn. Before he handed it to me, he said, "Let's hear it for our latest winner!"

Everybody started cheering and clapping for me.

I looked around for Mom and Amelia, but they weren't around to see me win. They didn't get to see the cheering and lights. I had never felt so proud of myself. I had never had so much attention. I kept looking for Mom. I wanted her to see me get my prize. I got a few pats on the back as the man on the mike handed me the unicorn. It was as big as me, and as I carried it through Circus Circus, everybody looked at me and some were probably envious of me. I had never felt so proud or so special. I loved all the looks I was getting. The more people looked at me, the more I smiled. I couldn't wait to tell Mom and Amelia.

When I finally saw them by the door of Circus Circus, Amelia had a small, stuffed brown bear and Mom looked like she was ready to go. "Scarlet! Where did you get that?" she said, scowling at me.

"I won it, Mom! You should have been there! It was…"

"Who gave that to you?"

"I won it, Mom. I had to throw red hoops on bottles and I did it! I did it!"

She looked at me and decided not to argue about it. "Well, I'm tired. Are you kids ready to go?" Mom was agitated and I wasn't sure why. "Amelia, I cannot let you out of my sight. You are just looking for trouble, young lady."

Amelia smiled at me, and we followed Mom out of Circus Circus.

I mouthed, "What happened?" to Amelia as I pulled tokens out of my pocket and put them on a bench for somebody to use.

"I met a cute boy." She smiled, then shrugged it off.

I smiled proudly, hugging my beautiful unicorn, and I was just glad Mom wasn't mad at me. Amelia always had cute boys around her, she had that gift, even as a kid. Mom hurried ahead of us, and we followed several steps behind her to our hotel. As we passed other people, children excitedly pointed at me and my unicorn. I was proud and happy until Amelia asked, "Can I have the unicorn?"

I felt like she'd punched me in the guts. I was stunned and could hardly speak, much less breathe. Suddenly, I felt guilty for winning the unicorn, but I didn't want to give it to her. I liked the way everybody looked at me while I carried it around. "Amelia, I love this unicorn. I won it."

"I'll trade you for this bear."

"No, Amelia. No." Why did she want to take this away from me? Suddenly all my good feelings had left me. I wanted to give her the unicorn, but I wanted it, too. I felt bad that I had this beautiful white unicorn and she had a small brown bear. I felt bad that I was getting so much attention and she was being ignored. Why did she want to take the attention away from me? I never got attention. "You can carry it, I guess, if you want to," I said, not really wanting to give it to her.

"Okay," she said, happily grabbing it and handing me her bear. Now she got the smiles and the looks. But for me, the magic of the night was gone.

I was disappointed that Amelia took my joy and the attention away from me. I'm the one who threw the red ring on the bottle, not her. I wasn't even excited to tell Tabitha anymore. Why couldn't somebody be proud of me, happy for me?

I never did enjoy the unicorn the way I should have. It was surrounded by negativity, and after only about a week of the unicorn sitting in my room staring at me, I didn't want it anymore. It didn't make me happy. It made me sad, so I took it to Amelia's room and knocked on her bedroom door. "Amelia, do you want this? I decided I don't want it. It really doesn't look good in my room."

"No, I don't want it."

I couldn't believe what I heard. "Are you sure? You wanted it after I won it."

"I don't want it," she said and closed the door on me.

I didn't understand. I had felt awful since the moment she asked me for the unicorn, and she didn't even want it. I tried to hang on to it. I tried to regain the magical feelings I had toward the unicorn, but I couldn't, and it eventually found its way into the garbage.

~~~~

I straightened Amelia's gown then covered her with the sheet and blanket. I had never really had a good look at her tattoo before, and I was surprised to see the similarities to the unicorn I had won, a white, rearing unicorn with a gold horn and blue eyes. I kissed Amelia's forehead and left the hospital. I went home and straight back to bed.

Chapter 8

AMELIA WOKE UP and smiled at Mom first, then realized I was there and smiled at me, too. "Scar, why aren't you modeling someplace?"

"I could be. Tell me you're fine and I'm out of here."

"Oh, Amelia, she doesn't mean that. Honey, how are you feeling?" Mom asked.

"I don't know. I think I'm on morphine or something, I don't really feel anything."

I rolled my eyes. *When has she ever felt anything?*

"I'm sure the doctors will be in soon to let me know what they've found out," Amelia said.

The more I thought about Amelia's condition, the more I knew, deep down, that it had to be her liver. How could it be anything else? If caught early enough, the liver should be okay.

And Amelia was young. I prayed that she had reached her bottom, and now she'd begin the climb back up to health and happiness. I'd get her into the best treatment facility. I'd rent a place for Mom to stay close to her. I'd get her the best doctors. And, thanks to my modeling career, I knew a few who specialized in addiction.

I'd get my sister back. Truthfully, I was looking forward to meeting my new sister, my sober sister. She had been a thorn in my side and Mom's side for too long. It's time we no longer had to worry about her. Mom needed a break, and I needed a break. I'd never felt surer about anything. I was convinced that this would be the wakeup call Amelia needed, and I was certain she would finally get the help she required.

I worried that the doctors were still giving her medication like morphine when her liver was struggling. But either way, I hoped she was enjoying it, because her drug use was coming to an end. I wondered how and when they would start her on this whole detox thing, curious to see how the treatment would unfold. I was anxious for Amelia to go through it, eager for her to get her second chance at her life. I couldn't wait to have a sober sister.

~~~~

I thought about the times I believed we were getting closer, like the first time she called me in the middle of the night, at two in the morning, and she wanted to visit. She told me about her latest boyfriend and how much he loved her. I found out she had just come from the hospital and they had given her a bottle of Percocet to help her with the pain. It made no sense that I would sit on the phone at that time of night, but for some reason I couldn't hang up. I didn't want to say goodbye. I liked that she wanted to talk to me, so I sat there on the phone with her until she passed out. Even then I waited to see if she'd wake back up and want to talk some more. I at least wanted to say good night to her before I hung up.

We had many of those late-night phone calls and, sadly, they had been some of the best conversations I'd ever had with her. In my mind, we were bonding, but Amelia almost never remembered our conversation. I didn't press her about the calls, I just kept acting like it didn't matter, and eventually stopped answering her late-night calls. Everything about my life with Amelia was irrational and disappointing.

And so I had a lot of hope and faith that this stint in the hospital would scare her into sobriety and I'd get my sister back.

Though I was deep in my own thoughts and tuning out most of their conversation, I did hear that Amelia had had several visitors. Her last 'friend' left twenty minutes before we got there. I excused myself and went into her bathroom. I looked through the garbage can, carefully pulling out the used paper towels, but found nothing. I left her room and went down the hall to a public bathroom, and cautiously pulled the garbage out piece by piece—and there it was, an empty vodka bottle. My heart dropped.

When I got back to Amelia's room, Mom was gone. I showed Amelia the bottle. "I know what you're doing. You either tell the doctors the truth or I will. This is bullshit."

"I don't know what you're talking about."

"Yes, you do. This is yours." I held up the bottle. "Your friend brought it to you, and I'm sure you had a good laugh

while you guys were drinking it, right? How we're all so stupid."
I dropped the bottle into the wastebasket by her bed, purposely
not hiding it. "You're the stupid one. And I'm telling the doctors, in case they're not bright enough to realize what's going
on. Or maybe they're just easily manipulated by you, the way so
many are." I thought about how many times I told her she
needed to take her life back. She needed help. She needed A.A.
"What's the point?" I said and turned to leave.

"Why do you think you know what's best for everybody
else but yourself?" she yelled to stop me and it did. "Fuck! Why
don't you look in the mirror? You're a model, that's it. And
you're getting old. You have no backup plan, no future after
modeling, and you've never even had a boyfriend other than
stupid childish crushes," she barked at me, hitting a nerve. "You
never do anything with Tabitha anymore. You don't have any
friends. You're afraid of your own life, you're afraid of men."
She looked at me sideways and said, "I'd be willing to bet you're
still a virgin. You have no life outside of the model monster and
yet you're going to attack me?"

I turned back and walked toward her. "You know why I
don't have time for anything else? Because whenever I have free
time, I'm pulled back into your mess. I should live in New
York, not Colorado. I can't make plans because I'm always tied
up in your latest drama. I'd love to spend time with Tabitha.
Having a friend that wants nothing from me would be a welcome shock to my system. I spend my free time either trying to
get close to you or trying to clean up your failure of a life. Mom
went from an alcoholic, no-good husband to having to deal
with an alcoholic, no-good daughter. Do you ever think about
her and what you put her through? You're killing yourself and

killing us in the process. Do you care? Do you care about any-body but yourself?"

"You just want excuses. You want to blame somebody. Might as well blame me, everybody else does. I'm always the problem!" she shouted.

"Now who's having a pity party?"

"Why have you never had a boyfriend?" she asked.

I wanted to say, 'why have you had so many boyfriends?' But I didn't. "I'm leaving. You tell the doctors the truth. Today. When I come back tomorrow, I'm telling them everything. Everything!"

Chapter 9

I WAS SITTING in on my very first, and hopefully last, A.A. meeting. I wanted to get an idea of who these people were. As they went around the room introducing themselves, I realized they were all alcoholics. "I'm Jackie and I'm an alcoholic."

"Hi, Jackie," the group said in unison.

"I'm John and I'm an alcoholic."

"Hi, John"

"I'm Teresa. I'm an alcoholic drug addict."

"Hi, Teresa."

"I'm Andy, a friend of A.A."

Whatever that means. When it was my turn, I said, "I'm... I'm Scarlet."

"Hi, Scarlet."

I was annoyed that they all seemed so happy and welcoming. *What, are they all drunk now?* I didn't understand the opening, and clearly, I didn't belong. In fact, I was pretty sure Amelia didn't belong either.

Once the meeting was underway, different people took turns talking various BS about their lives. "My son is displaying alcoholic tendencies. He's drinking and hiding it."

All right, this sounds familiar.

"I'm so fortunate that I'm sober today and able to see his problem so clearly. He's had A.A. in his life, because of me, for the last eight years. He knows where to go when he's sick and tired of being sick and tired."

I noticed everybody nodding in agreement. I raised my eyebrows in confusion.

Todd spoke next. "Todd, alcoholic. I have a different situation with my son. As you all probably know, I had a slip last month, which led to separation with my wife. Now my son is very angry with me and accuses me of having no self-discipline." He lowered his head. "He says I have no self-control. He's pissed that I blame my weakness on a disease. He said it's an insult to people with cancer, who don't have a choice." He looked back up. "He's seventeen, very angry and bitter, and swears he'll never have a drink. I hope it's true and he never drinks, because if he does he's got my genes and will probably end up just like me. This is a destructive disease and…"

I couldn't stop myself. "I don't know how this whole thing works… Maybe I'm out of line here." I held my hand toward Todd. "I'm sorry, I just don't get how this is supposed to be a disease. My sister has been drinking and taking prescription drugs for years. Now she's sick in the hospital. Is it her liver? I don't know yet. I say, yes, and then that would be a disease, right? Cirrhosis of the liver? She loves to drink and won't stop. She loves to make excuses to take drugs. She loves to be passed out on the couch. She loves to party with other scum, and she has no life. She does not have a disease." I tried to maintain control, but I couldn't stop myself. "This is her stupid choice. If she wanted to quit, she could, or get help to quit. But she doesn't get help. We've tried to help her. She won't take it." I paused. "If she had cancer she would get help. Whatever the reason she's in the hospital, she's there willingly and getting help. The addiction is her choice and she's not wanted help for that. She's manipulated her jerk boyfriends to bring her stuff right into her hospital room. I mean, honestly, now that you're all getting sober, I'm assuming," I said and looked around the room. "Who here really believes that addiction to alcohol is a disease?"

Everybody raised their hand.

"Well then, where does it stop? Maybe I'm addicted to modeling. And my mother is very sick with a disease, she can't stop reading historical romance novels." I pretended to stick my finger down my throat. "So do gamblers have a disease, too, or is it just alcoholics? And why do you get to label it a disease? It's a copout. It's all about not taking responsibility and creating someone or something to blame. This is bullshit!"

I stood up to leave and heard the group say, "Thanks for sharing, Scarlet."

"This is a joke!" I said and slammed the door behind me. If I hadn't been so pissed, the stupidity of them thanking me would have made me laugh out loud. I felt like I was in the twilight zone. These people were crazy.

My flip flops slapped my heels as I walked quickly down the hallway, then I heard the sound of a door closing and turned to look. A man from the meeting was hurrying after me. "Scarlet, wait."

"Oh, God." I took a deep breath and turned to face him. "I'm sorry about that. I hope I didn't offend anybody. I just don't agree with what you're doing."

"I'm Rex." He held out his hand to shake mine.

I didn't shake his hand, but I was immediately attracted to him and stunned by my strong fascination. He was taller than me, a little husky, brown hair, blue eyes, and a five o'clock shadow. "I don't have time for this," I said and turned to walk away.

"I agree with you in some ways... but I think you should hear me out before you judge another alcoholic. And it might help you with your sister."

"Fine." I walked over to a bench against the wall and sat down. "I could use help with my sister."

"Okay," he said and sat down on the bench with me. "It sounds like your sister has a disease."

"Why do you think that?" I asked sarcastically, but played along.

"Has your mom or dad ever had a problem with drinking?"

"I'm pretty sure that's why my mom divorced my dad. He chose booze over his family, so my mom chose her family over him."

"Many diseases are passed down through genes, such as cancer. That's why doctors always want to know your family history. Alcoholism is also passed through genes. If one parent is an alcoholic you have a greater chance of becoming an alcoholic, even if you've never been around him or ever met him. Now if both parents are alcoholic, you may have a tough road ahead of you."

"That makes sense. But why her and not me?"

"You might be, too."

I gave him a dirty look. "Whatever, I gotta go." I stood up. "Thanks for your time, but I need to go to the hospital and try to protect my sister."

He stood up, too. "I'm pretty sure the American Medical Association defines alcoholism as a disease," he said, as if trying to keep the conversation going.

I was annoyed, so all I could say was, "You know you have a mullet, right?"

He stood there silent, rapidly blinking his eyes. He looked kind of upset.

"I'm sorry, I just thought you should know in case you didn't realize it. I'm just saying you'd look better if you cut your hair short in back. I'm sorry." Continuing to put my foot in my mouth, I said, "The hair makes you look a certain way, like an old stoner, you know what I mean? I don't think that's the impression you want to put out there."

"What impression are you trying to make right now?" he asked.

Give me a break. I put my hands on my hips.

"You're right, old stoner is not the impression I'm trying to make. But that was rude. You're single, aren't you?"

Now *I* was upset. Everything Amelia had just said came rushing back. "I was trying to help you... look better," I said, turning and walking away. "Haircut. Easy fix." *Being single and not happy about it, not an easy fix.* Hurt and frustrated, I couldn't wait to get away from everybody. Thankfully, I had a shoot in San Francisco coming up.

Chapter 10

THE NEXT DAY, I went straight into a private office with Amelia's doctor. "We already know, Scarlet. We don't know how severe the problem is or for how long it's been going on. There's not a lot I can tell you without Amelia's permission," Dr. Windel said.

"Well, I can tell you it's been going on for many years, maybe since high school and it's severe. Besides drinking a lot of vodka, she's been on all sorts of prescription drugs. When she's turned away from pharmacies, she fakes an illness. She's very pretty and very manipulative, and she finds a way to get the drugs she wants and needs. Nobody would suspect that she's an alcoholic drug addict because she seems so put together, but she's a mess and good at hiding it." I leaned in closer. "Every day, there are empty bottles of vodka around her, little ones, big ones—I even found an empty bottle in her bathroom here, smuggled into the hospital by her friends. You're giving her morphine or Percocet or whatever, and she's still drinking." I waited for him to react but he didn't. "Look, I know you don't know her and you don't know me, but I'm telling you the truth."

"I talked to your mother, and she doesn't think Amelia has the problem you're describing."

"My mother is in denial and is probably a big part of the problem! My mother doesn't want to believe her daughter is an alcoholic or drug addict. She'd rather believe she's under stress or depressed and that's why Amelia's behavior is so messed up," I said.

"In fact, your mother felt very strongly that Amelia does not have a problem with drinking or drugs at all," Dr. Windel said, "and she warned me that you would have a different opinion. She was right."

"That's fine. You're the doctor. You make the call." I was so angry I didn't know what to say, and I was tired of fighting for Amelia when nobody else would. Maybe he didn't believe in addiction or know about it. Maybe I needed to talk to a specialist.

He looked at me impatiently, like there was something wrong with me, and said, "Look, I appreciate the information, Scarlet, and I'm taking it seriously. There's just not a lot I can share with you about your sister. You understand, right?"

"Yes, I understand. Is there somebody else I can talk to?"

"Like a counselor?" he asked.

I shook my head. "Forget it. I'm telling you the truth. If you choose not to believe me, that's up to you. What else can I do?"

"Like I said, I appreciate your time and we already know there's a problem. We're running more tests and we will get to the bottom of this."

Just then my cell phone rang. It was Mae calling me to make sure I'd make it to my shoot in San Francisco. I ignored Dr. Windel, left the office and continued talking to Mae. "Of course I'll be there. It will be good for me." The photo shoot was just an overnight stay, maybe two, in San Francisco that I had already committed to. I felt like I was going crazy and wanted to get out of Denver anyway. I decided to leave that night instead of the next morning, so I'd be a little fresher for the shoot.

Mae panicked about my already-booked jobs every time there was an emergency with my family, even though I probably had missed only one job because of Amelia. Mae just seemed to panic more often at this point in my career. She and I both understood the industry and knew that I have an expiration date. My twenty-fifth birthday was long past and I was moving in on thirty. Amelia was right, I was getting older, and I wasn't naive enough to think I could model for the rest of my life.

~~~~

When I began in the modeling business, Mae and her mother instilled in me that this career is usually short, and encouraged me to protect myself and my future. So I've been very good with money over the years, and I've managed to put quite a bit of money away for when my modeling career comes to an end. But I fear that day, and on some days I cry because I've built my whole world around modeling. There is nothing else I can do or would want to do, and on those days I feel like I'm back on Tabitha's dorm step, scared and wondering what I'll do with the rest of my life.

I don't know what I will do next. I don't have a plan, but I should be okay financially. I know I'll want to find something new I can be passionate about—a career that will carry me through the next phase of my life and, hopefully, the rest of my life. Sometimes I think about starting my own clothing line or modeling agency, but I just don't know. I'm not sure when the modeling will end and what will be my next step after that, and that scares me.

But for now, I still have the look they want. I'm the model they ask for. Everybody knows I give one hundred percent, because I know who butters my bread, and I don't take that lightly. I've never taken this career for granted, and I've never been called a diva. I'll ride this as long as possible, into my thirties if I can. Who knows? Maybe one day they'll want older models, or there'll still be enough modeling jobs to keep me somewhat busy.

~~~~

Anxious to get away from Mom and Amelia for a couple of days, I went home, packed, and headed for the airport.

Chapter 11

WHEN I GOT back from San Francisco, Mom called to tell me that we were to stay away from the hospital and Amelia for a few days. "They are putting Amelia through some type of detox and they'll let us know in a couple days when we can come back to visit."

"Thank God. Now do you believe Amelia has a problem?" I asked.

"They're just cleaning out her system. I probably used the wrong word, it's just some type of cleansing. She's been on medications for her back for quite some time."

"Okay, Mom." I said cynically. I wasn't going to argue. I was just glad they were putting her through detox. Mom also said Amelia would be working with a counselor, which I figured would be a counselor to help her with her addiction.

Because I didn't have to worry about Amelia for a few days, I finally had a break. I thought about going to an Al-Anon meeting, but instead I decided to visit Tabitha, who lived a couple hours away. I needed my Tabitha fix, and she didn't let me down.

Over lunch, I told her about my struggles with the doctor and she said, "It sounds like they're on the right track now. Even though it felt like the doctor wasn't listening to you, he probably was." While studying medicine, Tabitha had taken a special interest in the growing problem of chemical dependency and said if she could help in any way, she would, adding, "Alcohol withdrawal is potentially life threatening, so Amelia will go through shock both physically and emotionally."

"Wow!" I didn't know what to say. This was sounding a lot more serious than I had thought.

"I've seen it, Scarlet, and it's not pretty. It's awful what they go through coming off that stuff." She scrunched up her face. "I think, last I heard, the estimate was something like, half of all preventable deaths are related to addiction. That's frightening."

"That is scary. I hope they know what they're doing, and they take good care of her."

"They will. She's in a good hospital. Not sure I love her doctor, but she's in a safe place." She gave me a reassuring smile. "She'll be okay."

"I just want my sister back. I want a healthy, happy sister."

"Have you ever had that?" she asked cynically.

"I've seen glimpses, just enough that I still have hope."

"Remember when she stole your identity?" she said, opening her eyes wide. "That was crazy."

"Oh, no, don't remind me," I said, shaking my head in disbelief. "That was awful, and expensive."

"I know. I remember. I don't even know how she did it. She used your social security number?"

"Yup, and took out a loan in my name. Then I started getting bills. Once I realized it was her, I made the mistake of paying it off."

"Always trying to protect her," Tabitha said, and took a drink of her soda. "Well, I have hope, too. I hope this is her bottom. She has always been the most irrational person I've even known. Even when we were kids, she came across entitled, spoiled. Somehow she always got what she wanted."

I felt slightly uncomfortable about the way Tabitha was talking about Amelia, but it was all true. "I know. I used to think her irrational behavior was fun, exciting. I thought she was so wild and full of life. I looked up to her and wanted to be like her."

"I know you did." Tabitha smiled and said, "And I prayed every night that you wouldn't end up like your sister. I wouldn't have liked you." She took another drink then looked for the server, to ask for the check. "Unfortunately, *I've* become like her," she said and started laughing. "Scarlet, I date way too many men. They're all around me. I can't help myself. I've become man crazy, like your sister. Ever since my first love broke my heart, I can't stop, and truthfully, I'm not even that careful. I don't want to end up pregnant."

"Do you want to be in a relationship with these guys or are you just having fun?" I asked.

"Well, there is one doctor, an actual doctor, Pete, I'm crazy about, but he doesn't even know I exist. He's older, divorced. He's worldly and knows a lot about everything. He's kind of stuffy, but for some reason, I'm drawn to him. I would love to be in a relationship with him. There is just something about him…"

"Then I suggest being more careful with the fun guys, so when he does notice you, you're not pregnant with somebody else's baby."

She reached across the table for my hand. "You're really smart… for being a virgin," she teased.

I closed my eyes and exhaled. "I love you so much. You're the best friend anybody could have."

Placing her hand on her heart, Tabitha said, "I feel the same way about you. Love you. And I'm going to take your advice."

Chapter 12

WHEN I GOT back to Denver, Mom invited me over for dinner and to help her paint a wall in her living room.

"Gosh, I haven't been over here for so long. The place looks great," I said.

She rolled some paint on the wall. "Do you like the color?"

"Love it. Very romantic."

"The deep red reminds me of my novels," she said, and smiled.

"Me too!" Mom loved historical romance, but I didn't get it. I tried to read one once, but only made it through the first chapter and quit. I wasn't sure I'd ever really read a book all the way through to the end.

"You do the top because you're so tall," she said.

"Yes, I am," I said as I reached for the step ladder, "and you're not," I teased. It was nice to have Mom to myself for once. Knowing Amelia was finally safe and getting the proper help, I felt a little freer to enjoy Mom's company. I think we both felt it, but didn't talk about it.

"You mean I'm short… and pudgy," she shot back and pretended she was going to dab me with the paintbrush. "I'm so glad you girls don't have to worry about your weight, the way I've had to struggle my whole life to keep the pounds off."

"You're beautiful just the way you are, Mom." I didn't want to tell her that I sometimes worried about my weight because of my career. She wouldn't understand. We continued painting in silence. The joking was over, and it seemed we had nothing more to talk about, because neither of us wanted to talk about Amelia. That's when it occurred to me that Amelia's trouble was all we had in common—Amelia was all we ever talked about. To break the silence, I asked, "How's work going?"

"Great. We just got some new greeting cards. They are just so sweet. Lovely cards." She dipped her roller into the pan for more paint. "How's work going for you?"

"Good. I have a few shows booked." To keep the conversation going, I added, "I like to break up the photo shoots with runway. Keeps things interesting."

"Yes, I can see that," she said.

My heart was breaking. I loved my mom, but it was clear we didn't have a connection. We were not close in any way. My chest felt tight and I tried to think of something else to say, but my thoughts kept coming back to Amelia and Mom. Maybe when I started to detach from Amelia, I had pushed away from

Mom, too. The silence was deafening and I was angry at her for not trying to save our family. *I've lost my mother.*

I got down from the ladder to check my work. The first coat was on. "It looks great," I said. "I love it."

Mom used a smaller paintbrush to touch up one spot, then stepped back by me to admire her new red wall. "Definitely needs at least one more coat, but I like it." She smiled. "Ready for dinner?"

"I'm starved," I said, breathing the aroma of beef stroganoff that filled Mom's place.

Mom went into the kitchen and before we sat down at the table to eat, I looked around her place and remembered the townhouse when I first purchased it. Mom had done a wonderful job decorating, and though it wasn't my taste, I could still appreciate the romantic, feminine décor, seemingly taken right from the pages of her romance novels.

"How long have you lived here now, Mom? When did we get this place? Three years? Four?" Although I'm not smart, I am responsible with my money, and with the help of a real estate agent friend who happened to live in the exact community where I wanted my mother to live, I was able to get a great deal on this townhouse.

My real estate agent noticed cops coming around one of the units and assumed the place would be up for sale at a reasonable price. I had everything in order to buy and swiftly made a low-ball, quick-close, cash offer. The owners were a rich couple, who let their troubled son live there. When their son started harassing the neighbors, they were desperate to get him out of the townhouse to avoid further trouble, so they took my offer. After a little fixing up, my mother moved into her new home in the beautiful, gated community with great security. Now that she lived in a secure community, I didn't have to worry about her when I was away for work.

She was very surprised and happy the day I handed her the keys to her new place. It was one of the happiest days of my life, too, and it felt great to be able to do that for her. She couldn't believe it. I'd never seen her cry so much or for so long. For days she'd break down into tears, while walking around her townhome with the contractor, showing him the changes she'd like to make. She cried while talking to the designer about her ideas, and while the movers were bringing in some of her new furniture and some of her sentimental older pieces.

I was happy to see her move out of her small apartment in a rougher neighborhood. Her car had been broken into a couple times, and she didn't have a garage or decent parking. I loved that she was now only a couple miles from my townhouse, which I also stole with the help of my real estate agent. I loved getting a good deal and the art of negotiating. But I especially loved that my mom was now safe.

I would do anything for my mom and my mom would do anything for Amelia. So because Mom's place was a two-story townhome, with an upstairs master suite that she never used due to her bad knees, Mom let Amelia move in. She said she had no reason to use the upstairs. Instead, she used one of the guestrooms as her own, with a bathroom across the hall. She said she enjoyed living on one floor, being steps away from the kitchen she loved and her garden in the back. Amelia loved that Mom stayed downstairs, too.

For Amelia, the upstairs was like having her own wing of the house. She had a spacious bedroom, a beautiful bathroom with a big soaking tub, a huge walk-in closet and a sitting room just off the bedroom, which she referred to as her living room. She had a big TV, a stereo and a small deck off the sitting room. She was only missing her own kitchen and a private entrance. She was living large, but it was Mom's place and if that's what she wanted, that was fine with me. I hoped they could keep an eye on each other since I was almost never around.

I was sure that by always saying yes to Mom, I was indirectly always saying yes to Amelia, too. When I gave Mom money, she had more money to give to Amelia to help supply her addictions and support her lifestyle.

~~~~

After picking at my stroganoff in silence, I decided I'd rather talk about Amelia than have nothing to talk about. "Mom, why do you protect Amelia so much?"

"I love you girls. I'll always protect you." Then she smiled and said, "Luckily, I don't have to protect you. You've always kept yourself out of trouble."

"But do you ever think that you are doing more harm than good while trying to protect her? Maybe you're aiding her in not getting her life on track." I pushed a mushroom to the side of my plate. "If we are always there to clean up her messes, she'll never have to clean up her own messes. You know what I mean?"

"No, I don't know what you mean, and you don't know either. It's a mother's job to protect her kids."

"Isn't it a mother's job to teach her child how to stand on her own two feet?"

"Amelia stands on her own feet. She takes care of herself."

I could feel the tension building. "No, she doesn't. She depends on me, you, or whatever man she can get ahold of."

"Well, she's been sick. It's different," she said.

"I'm convinced that most of her issues are self-inflicted."

"That's ridiculous. And I don't want to talk about it anymore. You are so high and mighty with your modeling... you have no idea the struggles Amelia has had to go through."

That stung. I'd never heard her refer to me or my modeling that way before. "Yes, I do! You call me every time there is Amelia drama. Every time. I know everything Amelia's been through."

"Then you should have some sympathy for her."

"She gets enough from you. Don't you ever feel used, stomped on?" I said.

"No. She needs me and I'm there. Same for you."

I rolled my eyes. "You're not there for me. You've never been there for me. Do you know one thing about my personal life? Just one thing. Tell me one thing I'm struggling with right now in my personal life."

She stood up and paused, "Well, you're consumed with attacking your sister... I don't know, Scarlet! There is nothing wrong with your personal life. You don't have problems. You never have problems." She put the milk on the table.

"I do have problems, Mom. I have a lot of problems, but you are so consumed with Amelia that you don't have time to even take one glance my way, to see what I'm going through."

"Okay, tell me your problems! If that will make you feel better... in the middle of all of this with Amelia, why don't you unload on me, too? Tell me your problems! In case you don't realize, Amelia is in the hospital. In the hospital! But go ahead and tell me how bad your life is!" she said and sat down in a huff. "I'm listening!"

"It's too late. Tabitha is the only one I talk to. She's the only one who understands and cares about me and my life." I stood up. "I'm tired. I'll help you paint your second coat tomorrow." I turned to leave, then turned back. "Just forget what I said. You're right, my problems are nothing compared to Amelia's. I'm probably just tired. I'm going home and going to bed." I left.

~~~~

Being at Mom's house brought back memories of the last time I was there. Amelia lived with Mom, but had been staying almost every night at her latest boyfriend's place. One day Amelia called Mom and told her she was suffering from terrible back pain. Her boyfriend wouldn't do anything for her so she asked Mom to run to the pharmacy to fill her prescription of Oxycodone. So Mom dropped everything, got in her car, and drove to the pharmacy.

Mom called me, very upset. "The pharmacist told me that he could no longer fill certain prescriptions for Amelia because she has been filling them too frequently. He hinted at the idea that Amelia had a problem." Angry, Mom went to another pharmacy and was basically told the same thing. When she was finished venting to me, she called Amelia to tell her she couldn't fill the prescription. Of course Amelia told her there was some kind of mistake.

"No, Amelia there is no mistake," Mom told her. "What is going on?"

Amelia was so angry at Mom, she hung up on her. Mom began to question herself, thinking that maybe she had done something wrong when trying to fill the prescription. By the time Mom called me back again, I was on a plane on my way home from St Thomas. So she left a message, blaming herself for not getting Amelia her pain meds and worrying that Amelia was in agony, with a no-good boyfriend who wouldn't help her.

When I got home from St Thomas, I went straight over to Mom's, and together we went upstairs and ransacked Amelia's room to find the truth about her problems. We found tons of empty, miniature vodka bottles and large vodka bottles, and other types of alcohol bottles throughout her bedroom, stashed in shoes, purses, and drawers. We found an obscene amount of empty prescription bottles: Vicodin, Percocet, Darvocet, Oxycodone, Zoloft. That's when Mom's eyes were opened, but only briefly. I could see the terror in Mom's face as she got on the phone and called her doctor. "What is Xanax? What is Oxycodone? What are these pills for? What is Lunesta? What is Hydrocodone?"

I knew what most of the prescriptions were because I'd seen other models take some of the same drugs. I felt a sense of optimism that Mom could no longer avoid the truth of Amelia's addiction and we could get Amelia the proper help.

It was hard to watch her go through the realization of her daughter's addiction, but I stayed out of her way and let her work through it on her own. The doctor told her that if Amelia was a regular user of these drugs, to take her off could be dangerous. He said her whole system could shut down, with tremors, seizures, and body shock where her heart could stop or she could just stop breathing. Then I heard Mom say to the doctor, "Well, I don't think she's a *regular* user. And besides, she has a lot of pain from a back injury."

~~~~

I pulled up to my garage, and I shook my head in disbelief of my mother's denial. I was so deep in my thoughts, I must have been on autopilot. I didn't remember driving, but I was glad to be home. I didn't want to think about Mom or Amelia any more that night. I wondered if I should wash my hands of both of them. It wasn't healthy for me to be around them, but if I didn't have them, who would I have in my life? I had Tabitha. Mae. No other names came to mind. I grabbed my purse from the passenger's seat and saw an A.A. and Al-Anon schedule that I had received from the A.A. meeting I'd gone to. I picked it up and noticed that there was an Al-Anon meeting the next morning at a church nearby. I promised myself that I would go to the meeting before I headed back over to Mom's.

I walked into my empty, quiet home and loneliness set in. I wondered if I'd ever find a man to love, a man who would love me back.

Chapter 13

"SCARLET."

I turned and saw Rex, with a very short haircut. I couldn't hold back my smile. He looked sexy.

"Well, you were right about the hair," he said, and ran his hand through his short hair. "I didn't even realize how I looked. Thank you for telling me. I've gotten lots of compliments."

"You look amazing." I couldn't stop smiling.

"So, back for more with us powerless people, huh? How's your sister?"

"Um, no. I'm here for the other side. I'm going to an Al-Anon meeting," I said. "My sister…" I shook and lowered my head. "I just don't know what to do."

"There's nothing you can do. This is all on her." He reached over and gently squeezed my shoulder.

I felt awkward being touched by him, but I liked it.

"How about a late breakfast after the meeting? My meeting is down the hall, so I can meet you back here in an hour."

I wanted to say no, but instead I said, "Okay, but quick. I have to help my mom with some stuff."

"Done. See you in a few." As he walked down the hall, I watched him. His butt was not hidden in his oversized jeans and I loved his husky body.

The Al-Anon meeting was similar to the A.A. meeting except that I didn't hear one word anybody was saying. I couldn't stop thinking about Rex and his body and his new haircut, and I wondered and analyzed if it were even possible that he liked me. The time wouldn't move fast enough and at the same time I dreaded having breakfast with him. *What can he possibly see in me? Why would he be interested in me?* I wasn't nice to him or his A.A. group. I decided I was his pity case, and he was interested in helping me understand alcoholics, that's it. And that was fine, because I could use the help.

Rex jumped in the passenger's side of my Porsche SUV. "Nice car."

"Thanks. I splurged," I said as I drove to the restaurant.

"So, are you really a model?" he asked.

"Yes, but I still don't understand why or how. My sister's the pretty one in the family."

"I find that hard to believe. I'd put money on it that you're the pretty one."

I said nothing, but tried to hide my smile. He made me feel good about myself. He made me forget about Amelia for just a minute, and I liked it.

We sat in a booth and ordered our late breakfast. "So, what did you learn in Al-Anon?" he asked.

"Well, it might be a better fit for me. Somebody started talking about how alcoholics always seem to need a crutch. First it's alcohol to get them through life, then it's calling their addiction a disease, and then they don't want the bed they made so they hand it all over to God and say, 'Here, you deal with it.'"

He smiled and said, "I know you made that up, and it's kind of funny." He winked at me.

I smiled, too, liking that he called me out on my BS. "I'm not sure I paid much attention. I have a lot on my mind."

"I know you do. Keep coming back though, okay? Eventually some good stuff will stick." He took a drink of his coffee. "You are really set on the alcoholic taking full responsibility, aren't you?"

"Well, I have to be responsible for my choices, I think it's only fair alcoholics are responsible for theirs."

"Okay, but what if the alcoholics hand their lives over to God, or a fencepost, or a higher power, whatever they choose, and then miraculously they can stay sober? Would it matter to you how they got there?"

"Wow, that's interesting." *Hmm.* "I guess if the alcoholic became sober and happy and healthy, it wouldn't really matter how they did it."

"Okay, try to hold on to that, Scarlet, and everything else will fall into place. It's great to see that you do have an open mind," he teased then reached across the table to grab my hand.

It scared me and I pulled back, then quickly apologized. "I'm sorry, that scared me."

"I'm sorry, I didn't mean to scare you. I'm sorry."

I took a deep breath.

"And to give you a little hope about your sister, you can have a good relationship with her again. Once she gets this all figured out, you will learn to trust her again. Recovering alcoholics are the most humble and responsible people I know. I trust them more than I trust nonalcoholics."

I looked at him in disbelief. "That's the stupidest thing I've ever heard."

Rex laughed. "Sober alcoholics, Scarlet, not the drinking ones." He gently nudged his foot into mine under the table, then smiled. "You're funny, Scarlet. I like it."

I wasn't trying to be funny. My heart was fluttering, and I needed to stay in control. "Well, how am I supposed to help my sister? How do I get her sober?"

"You can't," he said and took another drink of coffee. "You have a support system, right? Somebody to talk to?"

"My best friend Tabitha, but that's about it. She's the greatest person I know, and she has a good understanding about alcoholism and addiction. She's a doctor. Plus, she knows my sister and our history."

Rex kept reminding me that there is nothing I can do about Amelia. "Only Amelia can fix Amelia. The sooner you figure that out the better off you'll be. You have to love her detached from her addiction and everything that comes with the addiction. You have to detach and protect yourself from the lies, manipulation and drama. Trust me, I know. I'm an alcoholic. My family tried everything to fix me, but it wasn't until they disowned me and made me fend for myself that I hit my bottom and got the help I needed. It's so hard on the family, I can't believe what I put them through."

He shared a lot about himself, and he wanted to learn about me. And every time my story turned to Amelia, he guided our conversation back to us. I couldn't believe how much Amelia consumed me and every aspect of my life.

"Well, let me give you my number so if you want to talk about this some more, or if you have any questions, you can call me. I really think you should go to more Al-Anon meetings; it might be better for you than the A.A. groups." Rex gave me a hug goodbye and handed me his business card—he was a contractor. Then he asked for my number, but I didn't give it to him.

Chapter 14

WHEN MOM OPENED the door to let me in, she said, "I'm sorry." She led the way back to the living room and I saw that the red wall was finished.

"You put the second coat on," I said.

"Third. Yes, I finished it last night after you left. I didn't want to have to put everything away, clean up and then drag everything back out again today, so I just finished it. And while I was painting, I thought about a lot of things."

I suspiciously listened. I had always believed her when she tried to get closer to me, and had always been let down within a couple days, when everything goes back to normal—her fussing over Amelia and ignoring me.

"I rehashed everything with Amelia. I actually went up into her room while the second coat was drying. Remember that day we found all those empty prescription bottles and vodka bottles?"

"Yes, I remember."

"That day the pharmacists were trying to tell me there was a problem with Amelia. You were trying to tell me there was a problem. My doctor was trying to tell me there was a problem. I didn't want to hear it. I blamed them for being heartless. I blamed you for being heartless."

I wondered where this was going. I was hearing something new and it seemed she was on the verge of telling me Amelia might have an addiction.

"I didn't want to believe Amelia had bigger problems than her bad back. I wanted to believe everything she told me. But I'm not sure I did. I felt like I was her only friend and if I didn't believe her, who would? You didn't," she said, looking at me. "And if I didn't fight for her, who would? If I wasn't there for her, who would be? So I fought for her and tried to stay on her side no matter what. She needed that, and I'm her mother. Who else did she have?"

"You're right, Mom, she's lost all her friends. But you understand why, right? She has hurt so many people. We can only take so much and then it's like we hit a wall. We've heard all the excuses, we've been used, we've been abused, we've been tricked, and we've been humiliated. Enough is enough. I just don't understand how you could take so much of her stomping on you and using you."

"I don't know, Scarlet. I just don't want to lose her."

"You already have," I said.

"It just hurts me so much when you say these things. Just makes me want to run back to her and protect her."

"Ugh. Here we go again. Just when I think we're getting on the same page, you do this. You do this every time."

Mom was silent.

I was silent. Inside I was screaming, *Fine! Run back to her! You're killing her! You're not helping her.* But instead I tried to think of a way to get us back on the right track. "Mom, do you have a problem with having a daughter who is an alcoholic? I mean, does it bother you to think she can never take another drink?"

"No, that would be fine with me."

"What if Amelia was a drug addict, would that bother you?"

"I just don't want to believe she has that, you know… what a hard life, to have that follow you around. I would like to see her quit or at least only take the medications when she really needs them. I don't want her to take pills because she wants to party or pass out."

"Mom, she is far from partying. She is not doing this for fun. She is sick." I wanted to find a way to make her understand. I wanted to make Mom change her thinking the same way Rex made me change mine. Amelia can hand it all over to a fence post if it makes her happy and healthy. I don't have to understand it. "Maybe if you could look at this like she has a rare disease and if she keeps eating green peppers, she will eventually die. You wouldn't help her get green peppers or support her trying to get green peppers, would you?"

"Of course not."

"Well, this is why I get so angry at times, because I feel like you're helping my sister, who I love with all my heart, get green peppers. That's why I'm angry at you. It doesn't make sense to me why you would help her kill herself. And maybe I'm wrong, but it's how I feel about Amelia and her situation. Amelia thinks she needs green peppers to live, but we know green peppers are killing her."

She took a deep breath and said, "If you're right, then it's time I make some changes. I don't want to grow more distant from you and I know we've grown apart. As Dr. Phil would say, 'How's it working for you?' I have one daughter who's always sick and a daughter who's always distant. It's not working."

I wanted to believe her. I wanted to believe things were going to change. But I still held on to so many resentments. We hadn't hugged for years, so I decided to give her the benefit of the doubt, and I hugged her. I was starving for her love, but I needed to stay protected.

Chapter 15

I LEFT TOWN the next day for a photo shoot. Mae was desperate for me to go, so, as always, I was happy to help. I almost never said no to her. Occasionally, I let her beg, but this was not one of those times. I was happy to get away again. Amelia was still going through detox, so I had time on my hands.

When I got back the next day, I went to an Al-Anon meeting, hoping to run into Rex. I didn't see him, so I was actually able to focus on the meeting. I learned a few things, and I was very inspired to hear some of the women talk about how they put themselves first and dealt with the consequences. That way they didn't have to feel such horrible resentment—they were taking care of themselves first. One woman said that even when she made her alcoholic husband the most important part of her life and always put him first, he still would hurt her. By detaching herself from his dependence, she was able to feel differently about him. She focused more on his being sick and less about him purposely hurting her, especially after everything she'd done for him.

It gave me a lot to think about as I drove to the hospital. Amelia was doing much better and could have visitors again. I couldn't wait to see the changes and hoped she could leave the hospital and go to a treatment center. Then it would only be a matter of weeks before I could have my sister back, my family back.

When I walked in to see Amelia, I was glad Mom wasn't there. "Has Mom been in?"

"Yes, she had to go to work for a few hours."

"Oh." I sat down. "So how are you doing?" I asked, smiling with anticipation.

"You won't believe what I've been through. I thought I was going to die. I thought white sticks were trying to get me. They were everywhere... coming after me. I guess it was mainly wrinkles in the bedding. It was so real, these evil white sticks. I'll never forget it. I'm still a little nauseous."

"Why were you hallucinating?" I was dying for her to tell me the truth.

"I don't know. I think they screwed up my medicine, but one of the doctors said something about me being on medication too long and they had to tweak that, and I guess I had a bad reaction. I really thought I was going to die. I was shaking, throwing up, sweating..."

"Really? I heard they were putting you through some kind of detox. Why? What was that all about?" *Please tell me the truth. Please!*

"Really? No. I don't know what they put me on but it was crazy. I hallucinated for an entire day. Seriously, I thought I was being attacked by white tree branches, white sticks. The sticks were all around me, but it was my sheets. See?" she started pointing at the rolls and wrinkles in her sheet and blanket. "Like this one right here," she said, then straightened it out right away. "It still freaks me out. So weird. But I'm way better now. I'm glad that's over."

"Hmm." I wanted to tell her that I knew the truth, but wondered if she knew the truth. Has anybody told her she's a drug addict, alcoholic? "I just don't understand. We were told to stay away, so the doctors must have expected this was going to happen."

"Oh. Well, and they wanted to get the alcohol and pain medication out of my system, clean slate to see what they're up against. I had been drinking a little more than usual over the last few days, because of my boyfriend cheating on me. I'm not really sure why they needed to do that. You know, I've taken pain medication because of my back pain, too. I think they just wanted to start over, fresh and new."

I rolled my eyes without her seeing. I tried to fight it but I couldn't stop myself and I raised my voice and said, "You are so full of shit! Who believes this garbage that comes out of your mouth? Do you? Do you believe what you're saying to me? Because if you do, you're more fucked up than I thought."

"What are you talking about?" Amelia said.

"I know what's going on. I know how fucked up your life is, and I'm pretty sure you know, too, but you're just too afraid to tell the truth."

"Wow, you're strong enough to carry that soap box around with you everywhere you go. Good for you!"

"You just think I'm standing on a box because you're lying in the gutter. I'm tired of walking on eggshells around you. I'm tired of fearing that I'm going to hurt your feelings or send you on a drinking binge. Or send you off to shack up with some dick. You're sick, in the hospital, your liver is probably failing and you want to continue playing these stupid games. You're crazy and you're never going to pull me into your crazy place. I've visited. I don't like it."

"Get out of here!"

"No! You're going to listen to me." I scooted closer to her. "This is your bottom! You are hitting your bottom right now, right here. And you're going to listen to everything I tell you! You're not fooling me. You're fooling a lot of people, but you're not fooling me. I know your lies. I know that every time you open your mouth you lie. I know that your world revolves around your next drug and your next drink. You pretend you care about me. You don't. You pretend you care about Mom. You don't. You only care about you!"

Amelia lifted her hands to her ears. "Get out or I'm calling the nurse!" she reached for the nurse call. I leaned in quickly and grabbed it before she did. She took a swing at me and shouted, "Get away from me!"

I pulled the buzzer farther away from her. "I'm not finished. Jesus, Amelia, what happened to you? What happened to you to make you do this to yourself?" I stopped yelling. "You need help. You need to stop this addiction that is destroying you. You, and this problem, devastate everybody around you.

Not only are you going through it, but everyone who loves you is dragged into it, too."

Amelia raised her hand and wiped away a tear, but she continued to look straight ahead and had an angry, closed-off expression.

I didn't know if she was listening or hearing what I was saying, but I had to keep talking. "Amelia, I think somebody hurt you a long time ago. I don't know if I hurt you, or if Mom hurt you, or Dad, or somebody else. But if I hurt you, I'm sorry. And if anybody else hurt you, I'm sorry. We can get help. You deserve a better life. You deserve to be happy. You can't possibly be happy living like this. Call me selfish, but I don't want to have to worry about you anymore. I don't want Mom to have to worry about you anymore."

"I don't want you worrying about me. I'm fine," she said.

"No, you're not! And the reason I know you're not fine is because every time you open your mouth, you tell a lie. So when you say, 'I don't want you worrying about me,' that's a lie. And when you say, 'I'm fine,' that is also a lie. Now what do you want to tell me?"

Amelia wiped away another tear. "Nothing."

"See, and that, too, is a lie." I squeezed her hand. "See how I got you figured out? You'll never fool me again. I know you, way better than you know yourself. That's why with us, things will never be the same. I'll never again enable you, and I'll never again let you fuck me over."

She shot me a dirty look, then just as quickly turned back to staring straight ahead.

"So, I know that one of your admirers was in to see you… What did he bring you? Drug or drink? Never mind, it really doesn't matter. And let me tell you why it doesn't matter—you'll lie. And, I could spend my life running around telling the doctors and nurses… or better yet, I could get a cot and spend every minute of every day with you to be sure you're not getting ahold of anything. Let's play that out. I waste all my time and energy to try to keep you clean when you don't want to be clean. It doesn't work, does it? Besides, I've been around you enough to know that you would tell him to hide it in your bathroom or the bathroom down the hall… you'd find a way. So what are my options to try to save my sister? I could walk away from you and all of your mess and never look back. Which is probably my best option. And I can pray one day that I get a phone call from you telling me that you're clean and sober and you want to repair our relationship. Then I'd think about it. But the shape you're in right now is meaningful. You're in a hospital bed, sick, maybe your body is shutting down from too much abuse. Or, it's even possible you're faking so you can get some better drugs, or maybe your body has finally succumbed to cirrhosis of the liver."

"I don't care if I die! You're such a bitch. You have no idea what my life is like. I don't care if I die. I hope I die. Then I'll be happy, you'll be happy and Mom will be happy."

"You're so fucked up! You don't even make sense! You think you dying would make us happy? You have fuckin' lost your mind! We want you in our lives. The real you! We want you with us. We want you to succeed. We want you to be happy. We want you to have a good life."

~~~~

After my hour-long lecture, I sat in the hospital parking lot, dazed by what I had just done. It felt great to unload on Amelia, but then I felt terrible guilt for what I had said to her. She's in the hospital, sick, and I let her have it. I tried to convince myself that it was the safest place for me to be angry and tell her the truth. She had constant care, and she couldn't run away to get wasted or shack up with some guy. She might actually have to lie there and think about everything I had just said to her.

Chapter 16

FEELING A LITTLE empowered when I got home, I called Rex. I was trying to convince myself that I wanted to put myself first like the woman in Al-Anon; I wanted to be around somebody who made me feel good. But truthfully, I just needed somebody to tell me that yelling at Amelia was okay. Though I felt a nervous energy about calling Rex, the guilt I felt was unbearable.

The doorbell rang. I checked my face and hair then answered the door. "Thanks for coming over," I said.

"Thanks for calling." He handed me a red rose, smiled, and said, "You look beautiful."

"Thank you. Come in and have a seat. I'll get us some water."

"How are things going?"

"Well, that's why I called. I'm struggling. I think I made a terrible mistake with Amelia today."

"Oh?"

"I went to see her, and I yelled at her. A lot."

Rex started laughing. "That's it?"

"I really let her have it. You wouldn't have believed it. *I* can't believe it."

"You are so adorable."

"I'm serious, Rex. This isn't funny. I'm feeling a lot of guilt. I told her that every time she opens her mouth, she's lying."

"She probably is."

I liked that Rex was on my side. "She just kept lying to me, and hiding the truth. I knew the facts, and she was denying everything as if I didn't know the truth. I got angry. I don't know if she is embarrassed by the truth, or if she doesn't know the truth herself. I just... I feel I'm losing my mind when I'm around her, or like she's in outer space and I'm trying to get her to come down to earth. It makes me crazy... I snapped."

"Okay, so she deserved it."

"But did she hear any of it? Did it do any good? Or is it best to keep my mouth shut and just live my life?"

"Oh, no. She heard you and if the timing is right, it will make an impact. Don't beat yourself up. It was probably due time for you to tell her the truth." He reached for my hand.

I didn't pull back right away, but I immediately started sweating. "I know you don't like to talk about it, but I guess I needed a sounding board, so thank you." I felt so nervous and giddy around Rex. *This has never happened before, I think he likes me.*

"Let's talk about you a little." He tried to pull me closer, but I resisted. He laughed, then asked sincerely, "How are you doing?"

Such an odd question, one I don't hear very often, usually just from a server in a restaurant who doesn't really care, or from random people who don't know me. But to hear "How are you doing?" from somebody who actually seems to care put me in a position to answer honestly. I don't know how I'm doing. "I'm getting by," I said.

"You said you just got back from another job. So how did that go?"

I smiled, and for a split second I felt a little choked up. "I had a really great time. It was quick, in and out, but I ate at this amazing pizza place with a couple other models after the shoot." I reached for my phone on the coffee table. "I wonder if it's a franchise and they have a restaurant here." I did a quick Google search. "If there's one within fifty miles, I'm taking you tonight." I grinned and kept searching.

"That sounds great. If not, I'll take you to *my* favorite pizza place, tonight." He smiled and tapped my leg. "You're pretty slender. You have a good appetite?"

"If it's good food." I looked up from my phone. "But I do have to keep an eye on my body. I'm a model, paid to look a certain way," I said, and cocked my head a little.

He locked eyes with me and said, "I can't wait to get to know you."

"Darn it. Looks like you'll be taking me for pizza." I leaned back on the couch. "But first I want to know a little more about you. How's work going for you?"

"It's great. Every day's a challenge and I like that."

"What do you do, exactly?"

"Well, at this point, I mainly oversee construction sites. Make sure all work is going smoothly, on budget, on time. To most, it's not that interesting, but I actually really love what I do," he said.

"I like that. I like it when people like what they do for a living. Puts everybody in a good mood," I said.

"You love modeling?"

"Oh, God." I put my hand on my heart. "It's my life. I love it more than anything in the world except Tabitha, well, and my family, as messed up as it is." I paused. "I'm getting older, and I'm not sure how long I'll be able to model, so I need to start getting excited about a new career for the next phase of my life. I have no idea what I want to do after modeling."

"I think you still have a few years to go. You look great to me." He reached for my hand again and kissed it. "What about that one model? She's older," he said, trying to remember her name.

"Kate Moss?"

"Um, maybe," he said, and laughed.

"Well, I'm no Kate Moss."

"Well, you look beautiful to me," he said, and winked. "You hungry? Should we head over to Pete's Pizza? Luckily, it's close by."

"Sounds perfect." I assumed this was our first date and I was excited.

Rex was a perfect gentleman. He opened doors for me and shared stories about his work, and in turn, I shared stories about my work. He wanted to get to know me, which made me feel important.

Surprisingly, the topic of Amelia didn't come up over pizza at all. And we didn't talk about his alcoholism either. It was like a normal date with two people getting to know each other. It was one the best nights of my life—having a man actually want to be with me. And I'll never forget his hug good night. He was so strong and confident. I sensed he would take care of me, look out for me, and protect me.

Chapter 17

I GOT A call from Mom early the next morning. She was crying. She said they wanted us at the hospital at ten for a family meeting with the doctors. It seemed they had test results, and we needed to weigh our options.

"What does that mean? Weigh our options. What does that mean?"

"I don't know, honey. But it doesn't sound good to me. I'm scared."

I pulled myself together and said, "I'm sure they just phrased it wrong. Maybe they want to know if she's going home with you or with me, you know, who can take better care of her while she's recovering. I guess we'll find out soon." I hoped they wanted us to decide which treatment center we wanted to send her to, but I had a knot in my stomach.

When I got to the hospital, Mom was already there in Amelia's room, but Amelia was gone. "Where is she?"

"I don't know," Mom said, but then Dr. Windel came in, pushing Amelia in a wheelchair.

"We just had a serious talk, and Amelia asked me to be here when she talks to you."

Thank God. At least if he's here, we'll get the truth.

Amelia, fighting tears, said, "Kidney failure—I need a kidney. My kidneys aren't functioning and I have to start dialysis. I guess it's pretty serious. I might die."

I heard Mom start to wail as she rocked back and forth, tears streaming down her face. I was shocked. "Are you sure?" I asked the doctor. "She doesn't seem that sick."

"Yes, we're sure. She's on the donor list, but as you probably know, it's a long list. And your sister doesn't have a lot of time, so our best bet is to get her on dialysis right away and see if either of you is a match."

"Yes, of course," I said. "When and how do we do it?"

"We'll need blood and urine. Your blood type will need to be a match, or be type O. We'll match HLAs, antigen matches and mismatches. Even if you're the right blood type, we have to do a cross-match to be sure her body won't attack and reject the kidney. We'll have the team interpret all of the results before we can give the green light. It will take about a week, maybe longer, before we will know. We'll probably do some follow-up tests, an EKG, medical history and psychological evaluation. If we get that far, then there will be a CT scan and an intravenous pyelography dye test, probably a few others, all relatively simple, painless tests. But we'll start with blood. We've scheduled you both for a blood draw this afternoon. We'll get the ball rolling.

Don't think too much about this. One small step at a time. Before we get too deep into this, we have to find out if either of you are even a match, okay? We have other options, but we want to move as quickly as we can for your daughter's, sister's sake," he said, looking first at Mom and then at me.

I left the hospital feeling numb. *This can't be happening. It can't be this serious.*

When I got home, I Googled everything I could find on kidneys, alcoholism, dialysis and transplants. Not knowing what I could trust on the internet, I tried to stay close to websites of famous medical centers like the Mayo Clinic and Cleveland Clinic, and places like the Hazelden Betty Ford Foundation. I found many papers written on chemical dependency and kidney failure, which confused me even more because I didn't understand the language and medical terms. So I emailed some links to Tabitha hoping that she could explain some of it to me so I could understand what was happening to my sister. Deep down, I knew I was searching for a reason not to give Amelia my kidney. I was scared—scared for Amelia, and scared for me and Mom.

That afternoon, after giving blood and urine, I went in to see Amelia. There was a woman in her room talking to her. I could tell she wasn't one of Amelia's friends. "I'm sorry, I didn't know you had company."

"Scar, you can come in," Amelia said.

I used to love when she called me Scar, but now all I could think about was having scars from giving my kidney, putting an end to my modeling career. I knew I couldn't model forever, but I wanted to be in control of when and how I quit. I felt my choices being taken away, with Amelia now in control of my life and my future.

As I walked in, the middle-aged woman nodded hello to me. She was nicely dressed, with her glasses resting on her nose as she took notes and kept talking to Amelia. "Have you ever done Spice?"

"Um, I think I might have."

"It mimics pot," she said, trying to see if Amelia remembered. "We've been seeing it around, and it causes havoc on the body, especially the kidneys."

"Scar, this is Dr. Pape. She is a counselor and helps people with addiction problems. She's concerned about me having an addiction." Amelia rolled her eyes. "Yes, I've taken a lot of medications, and I've done my share of drinking, but I don't have a problem, an addiction. The doctors want to make sure I'm fine before we do the transplant."

I wondered if this was part of the psych exam. Last night while I was Googling, I read that addicts had to be sober for at least six months before they could receive a donated organ. I didn't know if it was true or if family donation went by the same rule. I knew Amelia was trying to get me to tell Dr. Pape that she didn't have a problem. *If I lie, Amelia can get the needed kidney, but if I tell the truth, Amelia can't get the transplant.*

"Amelia, are you sure you want your sister listening in? We're talking about some personal issues," Dr. Pape asked.

"I'm sure. If we're a match, she's giving me her kidney," Amelia said. "She can stay."

I pushed a chair back against the wall and listened.

"I'm going to need you to sign a release stating that I can talk openly with Scarlet," Dr. Pape said, and pulled out some papers from her briefcase.

"Gladly," Amelia said, then signed the release and smiled at me.

"Okay, where were we?" Dr. Pape asked. "Has anybody ever been concerned about your drinking or drug use?"

"Well," she thought for a minute. "Just Scarlet. All my friends party like me, but they don't have the health issues I have, so they don't need pain medication the way I need it."

"Have you ever tried to quit drinking or taking drugs? Have you ever felt like you had a problem?"

"No, I haven't. I don't have a problem. But I did go to a doctor once in New Mexico and she told me I was going to die if I didn't quit. She was a quack."

"Well, I'm here to tell you that if you don't quit, you're going to die. That doctor was not a quack. Amelia, you are very sick..."

Amelia angrily looked at me. "Scarlet, leave!" she demanded and wiped a tear from her cheek.

I stayed seated.

"Amelia, you're in for the fight of your life. And I mean this is life or death."

"Who do you think you are? You don't know me or what I'm going through."

"Yes, I know everything about you. I have all your medical records and all the recent test results. I know the damage you've done to your body. But I want you to know, I don't care how you got to me. I wouldn't care if it was court ordered or your family dragged you to me, I don't care. All I care about is that I have you now. You're under my care, and I'm going to help you through this."

"I don't have a problem. I could quit partying if I wanted to, but I don't want to. And I need the medication because of my back pain. I don't have a problem."

"Do you ever take pain meds when you're not having pain?"

"I don't want to feel pain, that's why I take them. I don't wait until I'm in pain. That doesn't even make sense."

"Okay, Amelia, but does partying ever get old? Do you sometimes wish you were spending your time in a different way? Maybe with different people?"

Amelia shrugged while wiping away her tears.

"Well, have you ever wanted to change something in your life?" Dr. Pape handed her the box of tissue. "If you could change one thing, what would it be?"

After a long silence, Amelia said, "I wish I could start all over again." She took a Kleenex and wiped her nose.

"You can, Amelia. And I can help you." Dr. Pape reached over and patted Amelia's arm. "Tell me what you want your future to look like."

Amelia seemed to be searching for an answer, but only shrugged her shoulders again.

"Let me put it like this, if you had a daughter in your shoes, what would you want for her?"

Amelia looked at me, then said, "I'm tired. I don't want to talk anymore."

I knew exactly where Amelia's mind went—to our big secret—to the baby she lost. Suddenly I could see the guilt she felt for losing her baby, and I wondered if she had been using while she was pregnant.

"It's okay, Amelia. Just think about some of the things we've talked about. Think about your future and what you want," Dr. Pape said. "I want to leave you with something else to think about." She started putting away her pen and notebook and said, "We're as sick as our secrets. Those hidden pains and secrets come out in other ways, destructive ways." She stood up and moved her chair back. "And if you truly believe that Scarlet is the only person who thinks you have a problem, then Scarlet is the one person who has your back. She is the one person you can depend on."

She hit a nerve, and I wiped a tear from my cheek.

Dr. Pape looked at me and said, "Scarlet, I know you're frustrated, and you don't want to hear this." She looked back to Amelia and said, "But Amelia, you need the truth. You need to start telling the truth, and you need to hear the truth. It's what will save you. You need to keep Scarlet close to you."

Great. Dr. Pape's right. Not what I want to hear.

Amelia quietly said, "I'm in a lot of pain."

"I know you are." She reached over and gave Amelia's leg a loving squeeze. "We're going to get you the help you need. Is it okay if Scarlet and I go for a walk and talk? I believe she is willing to risk your relationship to be a true friend to you right now. Those are the people we need around you. We need her in your corner."

"I don't care."

Dr. Pape motioned for me to join her, so I followed her down the hall to a family waiting room that was empty, and we started to talk about Amelia's problems. "Well, your sister went through horrible withdrawal, and she's in a fight for her life. The prognosis isn't good. I believe she has a serious addiction to alcohol and prescription drugs, but I'm sure you already know that."

I nodded.

"As you know, her kidneys are failing, she's damaged her liver, and her stomach is a mess. I know where she is in her addiction, and I know she's going to resist treatment and counseling."

"I have to know something, Dr. Pape. Has Amelia brought this kidney failure on herself by abusing her body?" I asked.

"I can't answer that question. But I can tell you that what she's been doing has made everything worse. I don't know if she was predisposed to kidney failure, or if other factors played a role. I do know that alcohol abuse and drug abuse is very hard on the kidneys and liver."

"I read something about how alcohol dehydrates the body and dehydration can cause your kidneys to work harder than they should," I said, giving her a questioning look. "I thought if she's dehydrated, she'll drink more and you know… vicious cycle." Then I quickly added, "Is this her bottom? Is this when she will finally get her life back?"

"Like I said, she has a tough road ahead of her, and she is very sick. Sadly, Scarlet, there are only three options your sister has. She can drink and drug until she's dead. She can drink and drug until she is locked up, either in prison or a mental health institution. Or she can get sober and live her life. And the odds for all three are dead even—many choose death. And at the moment, Amelia is headed in that direction."

I didn't believe that Amelia was headed toward death. "I always wondered when she would be sick enough that she hit bottom, when she would be miserable enough that she'd be ready to get help. I hope this is it." I folded my hands as if praying. "I've tried to help her many times, and I've been through so much with her that my resentment and frustration is pretty obvious. Our relationship isn't healthy, and I'm angry. I know you said she needs me in her corner, but I've been in her corner for so long I'm worn out. I've kind of stepped back because it's too painful to watch and participate in her misery. I don't think my being in her life is good for either one of us." I crossed my arms in front of my chest and continued. "I tried to tell her doctor, but he didn't take me seriously. He believed her, not me."

"He did take you seriously, and I know he already knew Amelia had other issues going on. This addiction misunderstanding between doctors and substance abuse counselors is getting better, but medical doctors just don't understand addiction. They think nothing of prescribing pain killers because it's easier for them to write a prescription than to actually try to help the patient."

"Do the doctors get a kickback for prescribing certain drugs?" I interrupted.

She took a deep breath in frustration. "I don't know about that, but I've seen so many mistakes… I've heard doctors tell patients to drink a glass of red wine every night without bothering to ask the patient about their family and medical history."

"Isn't it frustrating trying to help people with addictions when the doctors won't help?"

She put her briefcase on the floor next to her. "I think we're finally starting to realize how dangerous and painful this disease is, medical doctors included. Sadly, it took the death of some celebrities for doctors to face the problem and be held accountable for over-prescribing certain drugs."

"So what is the game plan? She'll get dialysis, continue counseling with you, and just wait for a kidney?" I asked.

"The only way she will succeed is if she is motivated to change, and it *has* to be patient motivated. We could talk until we're blue in the face, but if she doesn't want to change, there's nothing we can do. This is not a curable condition, it's a chronic, lifelong disorder."

"I really have my doubts that she can change. I'm so angry at her sometimes." I said, feeling defeated.

"Don't be mad at Amelia—be mad at the disease. This disease has probably taken her to places she never thought she would go. She has a lot of shame in her heart. And it's all the disease. It's not Amelia hurting you, it's the disease."

"I have a really hard time calling it a disease, Dr. Pape. If you have cancer, you fight it. You go to the doctor and try to save your life. But if you have an addiction, you fight against the available help. You don't seem to care about saving your own life."

"Addicts care about their lives, but they are in so much pain, death doesn't seem like a bad option."

"Well, Amelia fully participates in her own illness and makes it sound like she just likes to party. Seems she doesn't care about anybody but herself."

"She can't care about anyone else, Scarlet. That's the disease. And let me assure you that she doesn't care about herself. The only thing she cares about is getting drunk or high to ease the emotional pain she's feeling. Your sister is in a lot of pain and that was the first truthful thing she said to me. I believe your sister feels very alone and lonely."

I knew that feeling too well, and it broke my heart to think that Amelia felt that way, too. It didn't make sense. She always had friends and boyfriends. How could she be lonely?

Dr. Pape wanted to get back to Amelia, so when I got to my car, I called Mae and told her to find me a job as quickly as possible. I didn't care what it was or how much it paid. I needed to get out of there. I needed to get away. I needed to get back to the one thing that filled me up and made me feel good about myself. I needed to block out Amelia.

Chapter 18

ON THE PLANE, I kept thinking about that smile, that slight smug smile that Amelia had every time she got something she wanted, every time I jumped at her command. I tried to remember if she'd had that same smile when I said, "Yes, of course..." about testing our kidneys. Or when she told Dr. Pape, "If we're a match, Scarlet's going to give me her kidney," then signed the release so Dr. Pape could talk to me. I just couldn't remember, but, I was convinced, she did.

When I got to the shoot, I was surprised to learn that I would be nude. In makeup, an artist painted my body to look like part of a detailed map. Five other models and I would lie side-by-side to create the complete map of the United States. I was painted white with black lines separating each state and areas of blue for lakes and rivers. I tried to imagine what this would look like if I had scars across my side and back. Could they alter the photo so the scars didn't show, or would it be easier to just get a different model?

When we were done, I went straight back to my hotel room and turned on the TV. I had a terrible headache and felt like I was starting to come down with something. I got into my pajamas, then called for room service. I ordered dinner along with two large glasses of orange juice. Snuggled into bed, I started flipping through the channels and was inundated by stories featuring addiction. There was a special on Michael Jackson on one channel; the Anna Nicole Smith story on Lifetime; and a report about the guy who played Truman Capote in *Capote*, who had apparently died of a heroin overdose, was on the news. A doctor being interviewed said that eighty percent of heroin addicts started using heroin because they could no longer get the prescription drugs they were addicted to. I wondered if Amelia had ever tried heroin.

I thought about the other celebrities who died way too young because of drugs and alcohol. My heart was breaking for Amelia, and for all addicts and their families and friends. I felt too achy to question why these people became addicts or why they put their loved ones through hell. I felt too sick to be angry, so I was just sad.

In my dream that night, Amelia was sitting up in her hospital bed smoking cigarettes and drinking vodka from the bottle. She told me how she always gets what she wants from me, even an organ. "I can take your insurance kidney away from you, and I can take away your career, too," she said, and laughed. "Who's going to want a scarred-up model? Who's going to want a scarred-up girlfriend with only one kidney? You'll be sick all the time and you'll never be able to have kids with only one kidney." She pointed at me with her cigarette and said, "Don't think I'm going to quit drinking and partying. I'll never stop." She took another swig from the bottle. "We're going to sacrifice you, so I can keep living. Truthfully, Scar, I won't be happy until you have been destroyed. I'm so tired of your perfect life."

I was crying and sweating when I woke up, and I cried most of the morning.

When I got back to Denver, I decided to skip the hospital and go straight home. Though I was feeling a little better, I wanted to make sure I didn't spread anything to Amelia or other patients. And, if I was run down, I'd probably be more susceptible to catching something floating around in the hospital. Maybe I caught my bug there in the first place.

At home, still feeling a little chill, I got into my pajamas and made some hot tea. And that's when Mom called and told me that Amelia had taken a turn for the worse, and she wasn't doing very well.

"What do you mean?"

"She's not very positive. She's depressed and didn't want me around today. They inserted something into her arm for the dialysis."

"Is it emotional or is she doing worse physically?" I asked. "Now that she's on dialysis, she should start feeling better, right?"

"Well, that Dr. Pape told me that if she loses hope, her fight will be much worse. She has to stay positive, but she isn't."

"Mom, I'm not going to go see her today because I'm not feeling one hundred percent, but I'm sure I'll be better tomorrow. So I'll…"

"Well, aren't you special!" she said and started to cry. "You're too sick to go see your dying sister." She hung up on me.

"...just didn't want to make her sicker..." I said out loud to nobody, and wondered how I had turned into the selfish one in my mom's eyes.

The phone rang again. Figuring it was Mom calling me back, I answered, even though I didn't want to talk to her. It was Rex.

Chapter 19

AFTER TWO CUPS of tea, a long conversation with Rex and a good night's rest, I felt much better as I hurried off to the hospital, hoping to cheer up Amelia. I planned to put on a good, strong front of happiness and positivity, in hopes it would rub off on her. Maybe it would make me a little better, too, and lift the burden of Amelia and Mom's negativity. Maybe it was time to change my attitude.

The moment I walked into her room, my positive outlook vanished and I felt defeated again. Mom was right. Amelia was depressed. She was sitting up in her bed, crying, and it looked like she had been crying for a long time. "Hey, Amelia," I said, trying to sound upbeat. "How's it going?" The doctors had inserted a tube into her arm, making me nauseous every time I looked at it. I was failing at hiding my concern.

"They keep telling me I'm a fuckin' alcoholic and drug addict and if I don't quit, I'm going to die. I didn't do anything with my life. I could have, I could have been something. I could have done something great, but I'm just a fuckin' alcoholic." She shook her head and looked down at the tube in her arm.

"What are you talking about, Amelia? You're so young and beautiful and fun and smart. Your whole life is ahead of you. I truly believe that. You can do and be anything you want. Your life is not over, it is finally beginning. For the first time, you finally have your life."

"I have nothing to live for."

I was stunned by the change in Amelia. I had never heard her talk like this. Struggling not to cry, I could feel the tears coming, because she was so sad and because part of me agreed that she had wasted her life. But I still had faith in her. She had her whole life ahead of her. She just had to want it badly enough to do the work, and it would be hard work, especially now that she needed a kidney. "I'll be right back," I said, and left the room before I broke down. I didn't want to cry in front of Amelia.

Upset by Amelia's state, I went looking for Dr. Pape. When I found her, I asked, "What did you do to her? She's depressed. I've never seen her like this. She's not getting better, she's getting worse. I think she's suicidal."

"Scarlet, emotionally, she's right where she needs to be. She's getting honest with herself, and it's hurting her. It's hurting her bad, and this is good. She needs to feel this stuff. She needs to face the truth. I have an appointment with her this afternoon… she's really opening up. Get her to talk, Scarlet, but call her on her bullshit. Do you understand what I'm saying?" She winked and smiled, then turned and walked back down the hallway, and disappeared into another patient's room.

I went back to Amelia's room. "I'm sorry, I just had to check on something." I sat down and looked at Amelia's swollen red face. "How are you holding up?"

"Not good. Do you see what's going on here?" She pointed to the door and said, "They're blaming me for having a bad kidney."

"Who said that?" That was news to me.

"Well, nobody has said it, but I know that's what they're thinking. They probably won't even let me be on the donors' list." Burying her face in her hands, she screamed, "Fuck! This isn't my fault!"

"What if it is your fault?"

"Fuck you, Scarlet."

"No. Amelia, I don't know if it's your fault. But what does it matter at this point? This is the situation you're in and you just have to do whatever you have to do to fix it."

She pointed at the door again. "They seem to care, and question if it's my fault," she said, wiping her eyes. "I just want a new kidney so I can get out of this place and get on with my life."

"What are you going to do with the rest of your life?"

"Oh, okay, Dr. Pape," she said sarcastically.

I knew Dr. Pape had been asking Amelia the same question. "Well, let's think about it, because I have to make plans for my future, too."

"I don't know what I'm going to do with the rest of my life. How could I possibly know that?"

"Remember that time when I came home from a trip and you were in the kitchen cooking and baking and you wanted to start your own business—bracelets? Do you remember that?"

"Yes. Why?"

"Because you seemed so different then, like you were happy. And I'm trying to figure out if you were drinking then or if you were sober."

Amelia said nothing.

"I want to know what happened, why you seemed so happy, so positive. I remember it like it was yesterday. You had dreams and goals. You didn't even want a boyfriend. You just wanted to focus on you for a while. Remember?"

"Yes, I remember," she snapped. Amelia took a deep breath. "I had just been released from treatment." She started to cry. "I was really sick. I almost died, so I checked myself in and stayed for about a month. I thought I had it figured out, so I left. That's around the time I was staying with you." She lowered her head. "I tried, but I couldn't help it. It didn't stick."

Again, I was fighting my tears. "Maybe you could try again with the bracelets. Maybe I could help. *I* also need to get excited about something. I have to figure out what I'm going to do after modeling. I just have no idea what I want to do once my career has run its course. I need a new direction, too."

"I don't know why you keep saying that. You're always booked."

I smiled. "For now." I stood up and stepped closer to her. "How would you feel if I brought your beads and things here for you to work on? It would give you something to do and maybe it'd cheer you up?"

"I'll think about it."

"I just worry about you and if we found something you loved, something you looked forward to, maybe you'd realize you have a lot to look forward to." I sat back down. "I just want you to be happy." I wanted to bring up another time when she was happy, but I was afraid I'd hurt her feelings. The only other time Amelia seemed to be on the right track was when she was pregnant and rescued that cat, Mystic. The big secret I was never supposed to talk about. I've never seen Amelia giggle so much or seem as genuinely happy as she was when Mystic was with her. I thought about getting her a kitten to help her feel better, but that memory of Mystic also brought a lot of heartache. Amelia carried her baby for only a few months before she lost her, and she then went back out partying. Because Amelia moved in with her boyfriend who didn't like cats, and I traveled too much to take care of a cat, I had to take Mystic back to the shelter. We never talk about that period in her life. I wondered if she talked about it with Dr. Pape.

"I'm okay, Scarlet. Just really sad. I hate my life and I don't think bracelets will help. I've been spending a lot of time with Dr. Pape. I guess I need help sorting through everything." She exhaled slowly, then said, "At first, the partying was fun, but somewhere along the road it wasn't as fun anymore. I'm not sure I've had fun for a long time. I've tried to convince myself that I was having a blast, but maybe I wasn't."

I moved closer. "You mean…"

"The drinking and partying… I guess it hasn't been fun for a long time. Dr. Pape explained it to me, the pleasure part of my brain became immune to the chemicals, but my need for more wasn't immune. I guess… she thinks I've wasted my life."

"I doubt she thinks that, and I know she didn't say that," I said.

"It still just doesn't seem real to me. How did I become one of those people?"

"I don't think *those* people are that bad, especially the sober ones." *Oh, Amelia, you wouldn't believe it. I can't believe it. This handsome man, Rex, likes me. He really likes me, and I like him, too. He's so manly and nice looking and smells good, and he likes to hold my hand. Can you believe it? I think your little sister finally has a boyfriend. Well, it's not official, but I think we're moving in that direction. He's amazing and I can't wait for you to meet him.* I wanted to tell her all about Rex and how he's a wonderful, non-drinking alcoholic, but I didn't.

"I don't have a lot of hope when I leave here. I don't think my life is going to get better. I don't know. I just don't know. When I leave here what do I have? Nothing. I have nothing. And I'll probably lose all my friends..."

"Amelia, you have to ask yourself if they were good friends. I'm sure you have fun memories with them, but were they truly good friends? You'll meet better people, better friends." I touched her bracelet on my wrist. "I went to an A.A. meeting and I've met some great people who don't drink. They would love to have you as a friend."

"I just can't see my life outside of this hospital room. I know I shouldn't go back to the way my life was, but I don't have any hope about my future either. What am I going to do? Who will I be?"

"Sky's the limit. You could go to school, sell your bracelets, or get a job. I'm sure if you're clean and sober you can live with me or Mom until you want to get your own place. You have so many options." This was such a change. Amelia always had everything figured out, and she was never wrong. It was the rest of us who always screwed up her life. But now she seemed so real, still confused, but real. And although I was, to some extent, being sucked into her mess, I had my foot on the brake. I kept tapping it wanting to slow down, not wanting to go too far into Amelia's chaos, wanting to protect myself from another broken heart. "You always have me. You're one of my best friends."

I let Amelia talk for a couple of hours, occasionally calling her out on false statements and exaggerated truths, until she told me she was tired and wanted to rest. I went home to rest, too, because Mom and I had to go through some more testing the next morning.

Chapter 20

AFTER ANOTHER BLOOD draw and a lot of questions, I headed over to see Amelia. As hard as it was to be in the hospital and go through the tests, I was feeling confident that Amelia would get better and this would all be behind us. I was looking forward to that day.

Amelia seemed to be in better spirits, but she looked tired. We made our initial small talk. "How are you doing? How did you sleep? Can I get you anything?"

Then she said, "I got some good news. One of the nurses said that maybe once I'm feeling better, I might be able to go home. She said most dialysis isn't done every day and that almost all patients go back to their regular lives, other than coming in for their treatment."

"Wow. I didn't know that. I hope she's right."

"They actually have me on a strict diet now and we're trying to figure out the dialysis schedule that works best for me. I think I'll start getting better," she said, and smiled. "And they are pretty sure I won't need a liver transplant. They believe once I'm on a better diet, my liver will repair itself."

"Wait a minute, I didn't know there was something that serious with your liver, or that the doctors were actually talking about a liver transplant."

"Well, a little, but they're pretty sure my liver will be fine."

I took a deep breath and wondered what else I didn't know about Amelia's health.

Then our conversation took a strange turn when she said, "Dr. Pape wants me to believe in a higher power. I already do, but I can't decide if she is preparing me for death, or if it has to do with something else."

"You didn't ask her?"

"No, I think I got too tired, I may have even fallen asleep on her," she said, giggling weakly.

I could tell she was tired. "My guess is that it's about recovery." We were not a religious family and had never gone to church. I used to go with Tabitha's family almost every Sunday. Tabitha wanted me to be baptized. She used to cry for me, fearing that I would go to hell if I wasn't baptized, and she wanted me to go to heaven with her. Her parents tried to get me baptized, too, but my mom didn't like the pressure and told them to back off. Tabitha still brings it up sometimes, so maybe I'll get baptized one of these days. It wouldn't hurt.

"It's so strange. Have you ever had an experience with God?" Amelia asked.

"Um, well, I know God loves us." I turned my head to the side. "I guess I don't know what you mean."

"An experience where, like, God has talked to you."

"No. Have you?" I was starting to get a little freaked out.

"Oh, yes, many times," she beamed. "Certain drugs made everything clear. Made me understand everything about love, life, and God. I felt so close to God. I felt like I mattered, like I was important and special."

Give me a break.

"Never felt that way straight. Never felt important or special. Always felt like I wasn't good enough. But then I'd be at a party and take something and I became one of the chosen ones. It was amazing. I don't know how to explain it. It's like when you meet a guy that you like and he makes it clear he likes you, too. You know that rush. It comes and goes quickly, it's like that, only a million times better. Like you're chosen, and it feels like it will last forever."

After twenty minutes of listening to Amelia talk about how much she loved drugs and the taste of alcohol, I cut her off. "I don't think you're supposed to talk about something so harmful in such an endearing way. This stuff has ruined your life and left you close to death! I can't sit here and listen to you glamorize these poisons. You are so delusional right now."

"You don't understand how drugs made me feel…"

"That's just it, Amelia, they didn't make you feel. You act like drugs or drinking make you feel better, but that is so deranged! That stuff makes everything a hundred times worse. People who don't drink see it; we understand how bad this stuff is for a person… Why don't you get it? Why can't you understand?"

"You should try it. Then you can lecture me. I love getting high, I love getting drunk, and it feels good to me. Makes me feel good about myself, like a wave of amazing feelings flowing over me."

I shook my head. "This is ridiculous. You're not making sense. This stuff has caused you nothing but pain and heartache and you keep defending it. Why aren't you angry at drugs and alcohol for ruining your life? I'm angry at it. I'm angry at the dickheads you've dated. I'm angry at the booze and the drugs. I'm angry that doctors have continued to prescribe drugs to you. I'm angry at everybody who has enabled you, including me."

"Okay, Scarlet, okay. I hear you, and you're right in a way… It isn't as fun as it used to be. I don't have as many friends. Sometimes I'm lonely… bored. I don't know what else to do, so I drink. When I'm high or drunk I'm not lonely or bored and I don't care that I've lost friends." She started rubbing the tube in her arm. "Everything is getting worse. I don't feel as good, I'm getting older and I know I'm not the prettiest, smartest, or most popular girl anymore. I don't feel that good about myself, and I want to feel good about me again."

"Amelia, take it easy with your arm," I said reaching over to stop her from rubbing it.

"It itches."

"Well, I'm sorry to break it to you, but you've never been that pretty or smart or anything great when you're wasted. To me, you were the prettiest, smartest, most talented, and engaging person during that time you were making bracelets *and when you were pregnant.* When you were sober. You can have that again."

"Seems all I want to do these days is sleep. In the last several months, I've been drinking and taking more sleeping pills than anything else. I just want to be left alone, so I can sleep. It's the only time I'm happy. I like sleeping away my troubles."

"But the same troubles are still there when you wake up."

"Yup, so I start all over again the next morning. I guess I'm trying to forget everything."

"What do you want to forget?"

"Too many things…" Amelia started to cry and shook her head. "I can't do this. You have to go. I need some rest."

"Amelia, I think you're amazing. I know you can overcome all of this. And if you want me to bring in your bracelets, you let me know." I stood up to leave. "Amelia, it doesn't matter what you've done or the mistakes you've made. You can turn it all around. Today is a new day. Tomorrow is a new day. I believe in you. I love you."

Walking down the hall, I imagined how bad it might be, being used up by men, maybe knocked around a little, doing things you would never do if you were sober, losing friends, and having lots of regrets. She can't get those years back. I was so sad for her that I didn't want to let her down like so many had before. I didn't want to give up hope, so I was prepared to give Amelia my kidney. I didn't care about the cost to my career. I'd find *some* work and maybe start a new career. Amelia and I could start making bracelets and other jewelry, maybe even clothing. Maybe we'd name our new business, Sisters.

When I got home, I felt a sense of ease knowing that I'd made the decision to give Amelia my kidney if we were a match. I was excited thinking about a new business and career with Amelia.

Although she hadn't committed to this plan, I was confident I could get her motivated about her bracelets again. It would be just what she needed, something to look forward to, and I was looking forward to spending time with my new sister and our future together.

I called Rex and invited him over. He said he'd be over in a couple hours, after work and a shower, and he'd pick up some dinner. I got comfortable on the couch and turned on the TV to occupy my time so I wouldn't impatiently watch the clock. I drifted off for about an hour. I awoke with a twitch, jumped into the shower and started getting ready for Rex. I was starving and couldn't wait to see what he would bring over for dinner.

I was anxious, but wishing I wasn't so attracted to him. He rang the bell, then walked in and set the bags down on the kitchen counter. Then he turned and gave me a long hug. Holding me tightly, he buried his face in my neck and kissed me. My knees buckled. He gently guided us, practically carrying me, to the couch and kissed me again. I hadn't been kissed for a long time, and I didn't remember what I was supposed to do with my tongue and I didn't care. I just let him do whatever he wanted. I lay back and he pressed his large body against mine. I could feel his hard penis against me, and that's when I stopped it. "I'm hungry," I whispered.

"What? Ah." He sat up and took a deep breath. "Me, too."

I sat up and smiled nervously.

He took another deep breath, then stood up and reached for my hand. "Let's eat," he said.

"What are we having?" I asked, though I was pretty sure I could smell Italian.

"A variety of pasta and salad... I wasn't sure what you liked," he said, and reached to give me another hug and nuzzled my neck again.

I didn't want to kiss him any more. I didn't want to give him the wrong idea. I liked him, but I didn't want to move that fast. I didn't even know him that well. "It's been a while for me," I lied. "I need to slow down a little. I'm attracted to you, but I just don't want to move too fast and make a mistake."

He quickly let me go. "I don't want to make a mistake either. I'm sorry."

"I just... I need to know you better. And I think you should know me better."

"You're different," Rex said.

"Really," I laughed. "Most women jump right into bed with you?"

"No. That's not what I mean. You're direct and clear, and I like it. I'll back off, but I'd like to be able to hold your hand from time to time. Are you okay with that?"

"I'd like that," I said, and smiled. "Should we eat?" We started to go through the bags of food. "Smells good. I'm starving." I was hungry, but with so much on my mind, I was afraid I wouldn't have an appetite. "Well, I'm spending a lot of time with Amelia and she's doing okay. She's starting to be more honest about her life, and she's very sad. At times today, I felt closer to her than I ever have."

"That's wonderful. Sounds like the counseling is working."

"Yes, and that's why I've decided, if I'm a match, I'll give her my kidney."

"No."

I sort of laughed. "What do you mean, no?"

"Scarlet, you're too young, and she is a practicing alcoholic."

"She's getting better and that's why I want to do this, but I'm not even sure it's possible unless she's been sober for six months."

"That's right, for a reason, Scarlet. If she doesn't stay sober—and I'm willing to bet that she will not stay sober—then you're throwing away your kidney, your career and possibly putting your own health and future at risk."

"Rex…"

"Scarlet, I want some say in this. I want to forbid you from doing it… what about us? What about our possible future together? What about if we want to have children? Scarlet, you have to think about this."

"All I can think about is saving my sister. I guess I never thought about having kids, but I don't think it would make a difference in *my* health. I only need one kidney."

"It's a serious surgery, and you just never know what could happen. I don't believe in surgery unless it's life or death—life or death for you, not somebody else."

"I hear what you're saying, and I agree with you about surgery, but we're talking about my sister."

"An alcoholic, drug addict sister who's never appreciated anything you've done for her. She's always taken advantage of you."

"Rex…"

"Scarlet, I'm falling in love with you. I don't want you to do it. I don't want to lose you."

"You're not going to lose me. Trust me, I don't really want to have surgery or lose one of my kidneys, but if you had seen her today you would understand. There were glimmers of change. Amelia is going to beat this addiction. She's getting better. She is going to overcome this, get healthy, and live a full and happy life, and I'm going to help. I have to. I don't want to lose my sister."

"What about you? You didn't make terrible decisions with your life. You have a great career, good friends and a bright future. She hasn't done anything with her life. She hasn't done one thing to try to better her life or work toward a successful future. She's only depended on you and others to take care of her and she's doing it again now. I'm getting angry at you. I can see so clearly that this is a mistake. I'm on the outside looking in and I'm begging you, please don't do this. Please, Scarlet."

"Rex, I care about you, but I don't know our future. I believe my sister still has a future."

"Are you saying we don't have a future?" he asked.

"No. That's not what I'm saying. It's just that my sister is blood. If I had the slightest doubt that she wasn't going to quit drinking, I wouldn't do it. I wouldn't. But I believe she is really going to quit."

"I think you're wrong," he said, and bowed his head. "I hope you give us a chance. And I hope you seriously think about your more distant future, not just the modeling, but your health now, and down the road." He sat down at the table and took my hand. "I'm not trying to get in your business, but because I didn't know much about kidney transplants, I looked it up online. There are some heartbreaking stories about the donors and their health problems after the surgery. It's a serious surgery and there's always risk." He ran his hands through his hair out of frustration. "How many times have you believed in her, trusted her, and she let you down?"

"Rex, maybe we should continue this conversation another time. I'm tired and I don't know how to make you understand. I wish we could agree to disagree, but I don't think we can get there tonight. I do understand that this is a big deal, and I appreciate your concern. I just don't want us to say things we'll regret."

Rex reached for my hand again. "Please think this through. I'm sorry I've upset you. I'm sorry. I care about you, and I'm scared that this could hurt you. I don't want to see you get hurt any more than you already have been."

"Rex, we don't even know if I'm a match. I shouldn't have said anything." I was starting to have mixed feeling about Rex. I don't like being controlled, I like making my own decisions.

"You're right, we don't even know. I'm sorry," he said.

No longer in the mood for company, I wanted to ask him to leave. But he had brought over a lot of food, so I thought of a way to let him stay without talking. "Maybe we should watch a movie."

"That sounds great," he said as he handed me a plate.

I filled my plate, then made my way to the living room and turned on the TV.

We barely talked the rest of the night, and I liked it. After we both had two plates full of the delicious pasta, I took the dishes into the kitchen, and he paused the movie. When I came back, he was lying on the couch, patting the space in front, inviting me to lie next to him. I hesitated until I saw him smile, then cautiously and uncomfortably lay down beside him. He wrapped his arm around me and reached for the remote to hit play.

I couldn't quit smiling. His body next to mine aroused me, and even though I told him I wanted to take things slowly, a part of me just wanted to get it over with. Tabitha had done it a few years ago, but that guy had broken her heart. I didn't think Rex would break my heart because I believed he really wanted a future with me. At least, he sure made it sound like he did. But then again Tabitha thought she had a future with her first love, too.

"Scarlet... Scarlet..."

I opened my eyes. Rex was still next to me but up on his elbow watching me.

"You fell asleep. The movie's over."

I was mortified. "I'm so embarrassed. I'm sorry," I said, sitting up rubbing my eyes.

"You were tired. Nothing to apologize for. Can I help you to bed?"

"I'm okay. I'm sorry. I didn't mean to fall asleep on you," I said and stood up, then stretched and yawned.

"It was nice," he said, standing up and collecting his keys and wallet. "You're very cute when you're falling asleep. Lots of sudden movements," he teased.

I walked him to the door and he gave me a kiss on the cheek. "Good night."

Chapter 21

THE NEXT MORNING I woke up feeling conflicted. I was again afraid of giving Amelia my kidney and afraid that I had upset Rex and he wouldn't like me anymore. I thought about a future with Rex and wondered if having only one kidney *would* be harmful for me, or to a growing baby. I wondered if I was truly ready to give up or restrict my career. I didn't want to be selfish about me and my life, but I was scared and I didn't know what was right.

Amelia's doctor called me and told me to come into his office at eleven that morning. So I pulled myself together and went straight to an Al-Anon meeting. I spoke for the first time. Up to this point I had only listened, but today I was ready to talk. "My sister has been an alcoholic and drug addict for as long as I can remember. Now she needs a kidney, and I think she expects me to give her mine. I mean, why wouldn't I? I've done everything else for her. I'm scared. I want to save her, but I've tried for years and I've never been able to. I don't know why I have such hope that I can save her life. I'm torn and I feel so guilty saying it, but I pray I'm not a match."

Marge spoke next and didn't say anything about my problem. In fact, nobody said anything other than, "Thanks for sharing." I wanted somebody to tell me what to do. I needed somebody else's opinion. I left Al-Anon a little disappointed that nobody would help me make a decision.

When I met with Dr. Windel, Mom was already in his office.

"Well, we have the results back and I have wonderful news," he said.

Oh, God, please don't let me be the match. Please don't let it be me. Please make my mom the match. I started to cry. *Oh please God, don't do this to me.*

"Scarlet, from what we can tell now, you're a perfect match. Like a twin."

I reached for a tissue from the box on his desk and wiped my eyes. I tried to act like I was happy.

Mom reached over and squeezed my knee, then said, "What about me? Am I a match?"

"No, I'm sorry you're not. We still need to do a little more testing and monitor Amelia. We're not sure she is ready for this type of surgery." He looked at Mom and said. "I'd like to talk to Scarlet alone for a minute."

"I'll be with Amelia," Mom said as she got up to leave.

"Okay, I'll be right in," I said, then turned back to Dr. Windel. When I heard the door close I said, "I'm scared. I don't know if I can do this."

"I know." He leaned forward. "I sensed that. Let me assure you, we have a great team. We've done many of these with great success and the match couldn't be better. You think about it. Come up with some questions, and if you decide to do this, we'll go into greater detail of what's involved."

"What do you mean if? Do I have a choice? Are there other potential donors?"

"There might be, but there is a wait and I'm not sure your sister can wait." He straightened his tie and said, "But, Scarlet, we also have to make sure your sister's on the right track, emotionally…"

"No offense to you, but my whole life I've avoided doctors, hospitals, and surgery. I'm scared of surgery, having people do things to me while I'm unconscious. I vowed to never do it unless it would save my life. I mean, I'm not even an organ donor if I die. I don't like the idea of changing what I was born with or cutting me up. And the thought of having a surgery that I don't need, losing an organ that I might need someday… what if I have kidney failure down the road… then I die?" I felt like I was going to hyperventilate. "I know I sound selfish right now. I can hear myself, but you also don't know our history and the trouble she's caused me over the years, and now this. I just wish it had been my mom, not me. She's not afraid of surgery at all. She's had her gall bladder removed, bunion surgery, shoulder surgery. Doesn't bother her. I wouldn't even get my teeth fixed when everyone in the business was telling me it would help my career—file down my teeth? Are you kidding me? No! Never. These are my teeth! I don't want to mess with what I have, the way it is."

"Trust me, Scarlet, you're not alone. Don't make a decision today. Think this through, write down your questions and let me know when you're ready to talk again. I can sense you're very stressed, so in the meantime, I'm going to give you a few Xanax to help you relax. I know this is hard." He started writing out a prescription. "You can get this filled right down stairs."

"What? No! I don't want that!" *Are you fucking kidding me!* I stood up. "I like to feel my feelings, not medicate them," I said, and walked out. I don't even like the guy. Why would a doctor suggest I take drugs… for no reason? *Fuck!* I left the hospital so furious that I called Tabitha and left her a message to call me. I told her it was an emergency. When she called me back, she said she only had five minutes because she was busy at the hospital. So I let loose and told her everything.

"Tabitha, I'm a match for Amelia, but I don't want to give her my kidney. You know how I am about surgery. Plus, I'd be out of work for quite a while and left with scars. I could end up a has-been and modeling is all I have. There's always newer, younger… Oh, Tabitha, the truth is, I want to blame modeling, but Amelia hasn't been the greatest sister. She's abused herself her whole life. I'm so angry that it comes to this, to me making this decision."

"Oh, Scarlet, hang in there. All your feelings are normal. You don't have to do it. Scarlet, do you hear me? You don't have to do it. In truth, I don't even think you should… I don't even think they would allow it, considering her issues."

With those words I broke down and started bawling. What a relief to talk to somebody who understood, somebody who knew Amelia and me and could give me permission to say no.

"I'll call you tonight, so we can talk this through."

"Okay... thank... you," I said between sobs. I hung up feeling a little better but still unsure about everything—Amelia, my kidney, modeling, Rex. I was trying to figure out how I would feel if I gave Amelia my kidney, and she went out and drank again. My hope was that she would change her life, but I had no guarantee that she would. What if by giving her my kidney I just bought her another five years of partying and nothing changed? What if my career was ruined, but her life stayed the same?

I spent an hour on the treadmill at the gym down the street, trying to sort out my feelings. I hated that I was a match and that I was in this position. I wasn't the right person to be in this position. I wasn't qualified, or smart enough, to make the right decision. I wanted this whole thing to be a bad dream. I wanted to wake up in Dubai and get a phone call from Mom about Amelia's latest drama... But then I wouldn't have met Rex...

When I got back home, I made a cup of Sleepytime tea, then talked to Tabitha for about an hour. "I'm scared to death, and I don't want to do it, but I'm sure I will. There's really no point in talking about it anymore. I'll sacrifice my life to save my sister and hope she doesn't let me down."

"I'm just not sure, Scarlet, that this is your decision to make. I don't think the team will allow Amelia to have a transplant, at least for a while. She's on dialysis right?"

"Even if I want to?"

"I don't know, but I think you need to talk to somebody and find out what is going on." After some silence, Tabitha said, "I can change the subject, if you want."

"Please."

"Okay, I had a fling with that doctor, Pete, last week. You know, the one I was telling you about, and now I feel like I'm going insane. I like him so much. I've been crazy about him for a long time, but now I'm even crazier about him. I'm trying to get him to ask me out or even acknowledge me… I think I blew it. I'm always friendly and smiling. I left a note on his car. Seriously, I'm acting like a fool."

I giggled. "I can't imagine it. He should be chasing you, not the other way around."

"Scarlet, you're the only one who thinks I'm special."

"That's not true. Everybody who meets you knows it." I took a sip of tea. "I can only tell you what I've heard other models say and it seems to work for them. Men want the chase, they want to work for it or it's not valuable."

"So I already blew it."

"No, but ignore him. Avoid him. See what happens."

"Ugh. I don't want to play games, but what the hell, I'll try it. What have I got to lose?"

"It's not a game, Tabitha. You're too busy to worry about what he's doing or thinking. That's just living your life. That's not a game," I said.

"I think you're right. He has been such a distraction. Thank you."

"But I have to say, I don't think this Pete is the right guy for you. He should already be chasing you, and if he's not, he's no good for you." I yawned. "With Rex, I think things are getting more serious. He says things that seem like he wants me in his future."

"Oh, Scarlet, I think they all say things like that."

"Really?" I smiled, feeling a little less pressure. "I'm just not sure yet if he's the one for me. I'm taking things very slow."

"And he's okay with that?"

"It's not up to him. But we have kissed." I sank deeper into the couch, trying to get comfortable. "I feel like there is so much going on in my life right now with Amelia. It's not fair to him, too much drama, but I'm glad he's in my life."

"Wow, he might be your first real boyfriend."

"I know. Sad, isn't it, at my age?" I took another sip of tea. "I haven't made out with anybody for a long time. Even though I told Rex that I wanted to go slow, and I do, I still sometimes wonder if I shouldn't just get it over with."

"Don't do it! Be with somebody you really care about, somebody who cares about you. I don't want to see you get hurt the way I did. That was awful!"

"Tabitha, you know I haven't had a real relationship. Rex feels like the real thing."

"That's exactly what I thought about my first. We are so far behind in this whole love thing. Remember in high school whenever a guy had a crush on either of us, we would avoid him and then secretly make up terrible stories and make a list of all the reasons why we couldn't date him."

I laughed. "That is so funny. Yes, unfortunately, I do remember."

"And all the other girls in our grade were having sex, but not us."

"Nope, not us. But I think you've caught up. I'm still so far behind."

"I think it will be Rex. I can't wait to meet him."

"I kinda hope it's Rex, but I'm scared of that feeling of being used. I remember the last time I made out with a guy. He wasn't a stranger but I hadn't really talked to him until one night at a party. We ended up in one of the bedrooms. At first, we talked and then he kissed me and next thing I knew he was on top of me, trying to take my pants off."

Tabitha giggled.

"When he finally realized it wasn't going to happen, he got up, walked out of the room, and left me there alone. It was so humiliating to walk out of the room alone after sharing some intimate time together. Ugh. What do you do, rejoin the party, or sneak out and find your way home? It's like the walk of shame I always hear about, only I haven't had sex yet... and I still had the walk of shame. That's when I decided I had to get to know somebody first, but even then, how do you know he's the right guy?" I stood up and stretched. "I think I should just get it over with. I'm going to call Rex right now!" I joked.

"Okay, do it. I dare you," she teased back. "You know, Scarlet, it just occurred to me that you're doing everything right and you'll be rewarded with a good life. Everybody would have expected me to have the perfect life. I have both my parents who have supported me through medical school. I went to a good school, and I'm working on my career. I don't always make the right decisions, clearly. I'm chasing a guy who doesn't want to be with me." She took a deep breath and exhaled loudly. "Then look at you. You come from a dysfunctional family, single mother, not much college and yet with all of that against you, you have made a good life for yourself. And you're still saving yourself for the right guy. You're not rushing to find a man to complete you. You're pretty inspiring."

"See, and I think you're the inspiring one. Don't let that guy screw you up," I said.

"I won't. Thank you. You're right. And I'm going to keep you in my heart, thoughts and prayers while you make these decisions. Call me anytime you need me. I mean it."

"I will. Thank you."

"I don't care if it's about your mom or Amelia or even if it's about Rex wanting to put his hands down your pants, you call me," she said, and giggled.

"You'll be the first to know when that happens."

"Good. Sleep well."

"You, too. Love you."

"Love you more."

When I finally went to bed, I was still hoping, wishing I'd wake up in the morning and the whole thing would be a bad dream. My heart was breaking every second that my sister was so sick and alone. I prayed that night for God to help me do the right thing.

Chapter 22

WHEN I GOT to the hospital, Mom was in Amelia's room. I hadn't talked to her, so I didn't know if she'd told Amelia that I was a match. I was hoping she hadn't. I cautiously walked in and sat down, sure that guilt showed in my every body movement and facial expression. I didn't want to talk about it, because I still didn't know what I was going to do. One minute I was ready to give Amelia my kidney, and the next minute I wasn't going to do it. I was confused and the confusion had led to a stressful, sleepless night.

I had always felt somewhat abandoned by my mother, so believing Mom wanted me to donate my organ without question made me resent them both. It seemed my mother expected I'd readily give Amelia my kidney, probably because that's the way things always happened in our family—I always did what Mom and Amelia wanted me to do. And I always did everything I could to make their lives easier, better. They were the only family I had and I loved them, but I was filled with resentment and guilt at the situation I was in.

After some small talk and listening to Amelia talk about how awful dialysis is, I said I had some things I needed to do and I'd see them later. I wanted to be held. I wanted Rex to hold me. I called him, but he was busy at work. I called Tabitha, but there was no answer. So I went home, kicked off my shoes and went straight to bed. Not even bothering to undress, I crawled under the covers and pushed my extra pillows up against me so I wouldn't feel so alone.

Before I had the chance to fall asleep, the doorbell rang, so I got up, hoping it was Rex. It was my mother.

"Honey, I know you're scared…" I sat down on the couch preparing myself for the lecture as to why I must give Amelia my kidney. "I'm scared, too," she said, sitting down next to me. "I told Amelia that neither of us was a match."

"What?" My eyes filled with tears. "What do you mean?"

"Scarlet, it should have been me. I wish it had been me. I know how you feel about surgery, and we don't know why she has kidney failure. What if you have the same problem down the road… You're not a match, Scarlet. You're not a match! Do you understand me?" She wiped away my tears, then her own. "You're too young and I will not let you do this."

I sat there crying and shaking, not knowing how I should feel. I didn't know what to say. I couldn't believe what my mother was doing for me because she had never stood up for me before.

"I told Amelia that we have to wait for a donor. Naturally, she's disappointed and scared, as we all are. But I don't want you to give it another thought, Scarlet."

Relief flooded over me, but the guilt was still overpowering. I couldn't believe Mom would lie to Amelia for me. "But then how are we going to save her?" I asked.

"I'm already checking to see if we can switch with somebody. My kidney might work for somebody else and somebody else's might work for Amelia. That's what we're going to do. It's called a paired exchange, Dr. Windel told me about it. That's our next step. That's what we're doing, okay? I don't want you to worry about it another second. Everything is going to work out. Everything will be fine. We're all going to be okay." She hugged me one more time and then pulled away. "It's going to be okay," she said again.

In that moment I believed her and I felt protected and loved, and I trusted my mom—feelings I had never felt before.

Chapter 23

THE NEXT DAY Mom and Amelia were in good spirits. An attractive male nurse walked in to check on Amelia. She kept giving me eyes like he was hot. She was giggly and flirty with him, and he seemed to enjoy the attention.

After he left, Amelia said, "There's one for you, Scarlet."

"I think he's a good one for *you*," I teased back.

"I've been a terrible role model for you girls when it comes to men," Mom chimed in.

"Why didn't you ever remarry?" Amelia asked Mom.

"No reason to. After I took some time to heal, I started to feel good about myself. I liked my life as it was. I had great friends, we traveled and did fun things together. I had my two crazy, wonderful girls who kept me busy and entertained. I loved my work, my hobbies, reading my novels, bingo, and my trips to the Blackhawk casinos. I have a full life without a man. Do I miss men? Sometimes I think about giving them a try, but I'm just not willing to change my life again."

"I hope I can feel that way without a man, at least for a while," Amelia said.

"I sometimes wonder if I had remarried, would you girls have had a better life. I just don't know. I did the best I could. If I had been closer to my own family, would that have been good? I guess I felt like my friends were my family, our extended family. We've had a pretty good life, right?"

Amelia looked at me quizzically, then said, "Geez, Mom, it's not the end of the world. Yes, our lives have been great, especially Scarlet's."

"Mom, remember every Halloween at the gift shop, how you made us all dress up like characters from your historical romance novels?" I said, trying to lighten the conversation.

"Oh, how I had to fight with you, Amelia. You always wanted to be a naughty nurse or a sexy witch, always wanting to look racy for the boys."

"My favorite year was when I tricked you and ended up as the town whore." Amelia giggled. "Hey, still a character from your novels."

"Mom was so mad at you, but I thought it was funny." I laughed. "So, Amelia, did that bottle you were carrying around have booze in it?" I asked wanting to know, but also wanting to keep the banter light.

"No! I was sixteen."

I didn't believe her. I remembered her as the town whore, and at the time I thought she was so cool and uninhibited, but I was pretty sure she had some type of alcohol in that bottle.

"I can't understand how you love those romance novels so much, Mom, but you never give romance a shot in your own life," Amelia said.

"Can we change the subject?" I hated talking about sex and relationships with Mom and Amelia. They were too open, and it made me uncomfortable.

"Dad ruined her," Amelia said. "Mom was destroyed by Dad's drinking." She looked at Mom. "Right, Mom?"

Oh, you're sober for a minute and you're now an expert on alcoholism.

"Not exactly. We were in love and I was excited about our future together. I knew he was the one for me, and I knew I was the one for him. We were partners in crime." She giggled. "But after we were married, I felt like I had been tricked. Everything changed. Suddenly my life became his life; he dictated how we lived, what we did, how we spent money. Of course, he made the money, so he had control over it. I just went along with everything and tried to be a good wife. I started to feel like wives don't have choices. They can't make decisions, and they can't have an opinion or a voice."

"Wow, then it's even more ironic that you read those novels. Aren't all the women in those books submissive?"

"No, they're pretty feisty. I like my books, and I love my life. My days are full and I don't have to answer to a man who thinks my life is his."

"That was in the fifties, Mom. It's not like that anymore," Amelia said.

"I hope you girls settle down and get married. But I also hope that when you do, that it's a fifty-fifty partnership. If you don't have a healthy partnership, there's nothing wrong with being single and having a career," Mom said, and they both looked at me.

"Seriously, you're both looking at me. Well, for your information," I said, "I've met somebody and that's all I'm going to say. When I'm ready, you can meet him." They both looked stunned. "And besides that, I believe that as long as a woman has her own money and her own career, he doesn't have a choice but to be in a fifty-fifty relationship. I'm not worried."

"I just hope you girls don't give too much. Give, give, give until you're ruined, worn out, and full of resentment. For some reason, that's what women do," Mom said.

Ugh! I've been hearing this from her for years—married women are left out of their own lives. They are not allowed to have their own hopes, dreams, and goals. He thinks his goals are her goals. What he wants, she should want. It is her responsibility to do everything with the kids, house, pets, etc. That's why there is so much divorce. It's not because of cheating and money. It's because women are worn out from their husbands. They don't have choices, and on and on. I was so sick of hearing her complain about marriage. "It's only that way, when women make it that way. Not all women give too much."

"You're right, Scarlet. I'm probably a little bitter. You girls should ignore everything I've said about men and relationships. I really don't know anything, and I was probably just with the wrong man. But at least I got you two girls out of it," she said, looking up as if thanking God. "Or maybe it's just that my marriage was not equal. I did everything his way and I just kept thinking, I'll do what he wants, I'll give as much as I can, it will be my turn soon—but it was never my turn. I guess I was afraid if I tried again with a new man, I'd run into the same problem, or I'd have to spend a lot of time fighting for equality. I don't want to fight anymore. I like being number one in my life. I like the freedom to do whatever I want whenever I want."

"Was Dad always an alcoholic?" Amelia asked.

I wondered if Amelia was trying to understand her own addictions better.

"Well, let's see. After you two girls were born, that's when the drinking got worse, out of control. He thought he had control of me, but he was beginning to see that he didn't. I put you girls first. So he started pushing for even more control. Then he decided to end our marriage, thinking that it would straighten me out and I would hate my life, have no money, and come running back to him—then he'd have even more control. But after you girls and I moved out, I got over the misery of my failed marriage, the rejection from the man I thought I would spend my life with, and the realization that I had serious financial trouble. I discovered that his kicking me out was a blessing in disguise. He did for me what I didn't have the courage to do for myself. Deep down, I'd wanted out for a long time, but I didn't believe I could make it without him. I also didn't want to abandon him, even though I had abandoned myself for years. What a blessing it was!"

"So he wasn't an alcoholic when you met him?" Amelia asked.

"Maybe he was, and I just didn't know it," Mom said. "He broke my heart. I did love him, but I just couldn't be with him anymore… the way he was. The drinking made him so manipulative and malicious with his words. When he could tell I was pulling away, he told me I was disgusting and that I'd always be alone. The joke's on him, because I have my girls, so I'll never be alone."

Amelia and I shared a concerned look. It seemed Dad was right, not about the disgusting part, but about the part that Mom would always be alone. I wondered if Mom believed that she was disgusting and so she never tried to have another relationship.

"To this day, every morning while getting ready for work, I look in the mirror and wonder what it is that is so disgusting about me. Then I pick myself apart. Is it my hair, my wrinkles? Do I smell or have bad breath? Was it how I slept? Did I snore? Is it the way I blow my nose? The way I eat? Every day, all day, I go through this checklist trying to find out what is so bad about me. Logically, I know I'm okay, but something deep inside feels really… disgusting…"

"How could you let him have that kind of power over you?" I demanded. "He was a loser alcoholic! You shouldn't have listened to anything he had to say."

"Yeah, Mom, you're not disgusting," Amelia said, reaching for Mom's hand. "He was the disgusting one."

"Gosh, I can't believe I just shared that. He stopped liking me, and I stopped liking me, too. I couldn't blame him… I can't believe it's been so many years and it still hurts me. Maybe I need to get some counseling."

"He wanted to make you feel bad about yourself and he won. You let him win," I said. "He was just trying to bring you down to his level."

"I wish I had been stronger. I really wish I was stronger," Mom said.

We talked for several hours, all about emotionally-draining family baggage, with some laughter to lighten our heavy topic. I was too tired to understand how it all tied in with our lives today and I wasn't sure I even cared. Maybe it was good for Mom to unload and maybe it was good for Amelia to try to get a better understanding of our dad. But I could tell Amelia was getting tired, so I said my goodbyes and headed home, anxious to get away from our depressing conversation.

When I got home, I checked the mail and discovered the hospital bills had started coming in. Besides Amelia's insurance payment, which didn't cover everything, I had three bills that probably wouldn't be covered, one for five hundred, one for twelve hundred and another for about two thousand. I would take care of them in the morning, but it was clear that I needed to keep working. I had to take care of my family.

Chapter 24

THE NEXT MORNING, as I was walking out the door, Mae called to see how I was doing and when I'd be more available.

"I'm available anytime. Just call me with a job. I'll be there."

"I don't think you get it, Scarlet. You should be booked solid, but you're in Denver. I need you in Europe right now."

"I'm sorry."

"It's okay, I know you have family stuff, but can you be in New York on Thursday?"

"Yes."

"Okay. How's your sister?"

I wanted to tell her that Amelia needed a kidney or she'd die, but I didn't. "We're still trying to figure things out."

"Well, hang in there. Maybe your sister should come with you, lift her spirits."

"Um…"

"Listen, Scarlet, I have to get going, catching a flight. Call me when you get to New York," she said, and hung up.

"I will," I whispered as I slid my phone into my purse and started my car. I decided to leave that day. I didn't want to wait until Thursday. I wanted to get out of town and away from everything. I wanted to spend a day shopping and eating out. I wanted to be alone, lost in a big city.

I left messages for Mom, Rex and Tabitha that I was going to New York for a couple of days for a shoot. I did stop by the hospital to check on Amelia. She didn't look good, and she said she was tired and didn't want to talk. I kissed her on the forehead and said, "I'll be back in a few days. Call me anytime if you need to talk. I'm here for you." I felt guilty for leaving, knowing I was a hypocrite. "I'm here for you" was such a lie. I wasn't there for her. I was running away to avoid her and Mom and the hospital and my own guilt that kept gnawing away at me. I was hoping this trip would give me time to think.

I made it to Manhattan and checked into the hotel. When I got up to my room I called Mae. "I'm here a couple days early. I needed to get out of Denver."

"That's my Scarlet! You wanna do a show tomorrow night?"

"Sure."

"Great. So nice to have you back. I was getting worried about you."

Worried about me? Why was she worried about me? I've never let her down. I've never given her reason to worry about me, unlike some of the other models, I've helped her out many times, taking jobs for less pay, I've happily stepped in when I was sleep-deprived and jetlagged, coming off a redeye. I've filled in when another model wouldn't or couldn't do the shoot. I've never let her down, or anybody else.

I called the front desk to connect me with the spa. I needed a facial or a massage. I'd even take a body wrap at this point. Luckily, I got in right away for a massage. While I was lying on the table, I started thinking maybe I was letting Mae down the same way I was letting Amelia down. Even though I believed I went out of my way for them, I was being made to feel that I let them down and they deserved better from me. I didn't know what I was doing so wrong in my life and why I was feeling so overwhelmed by the two things that I had given to the most—modeling and Amelia.

I tried to relax, but I was paralyzed by fear and sadness. Maybe all the times I helped Amelia, it didn't really put me out in any emotional way, just financially. And maybe always being available for Mae, which some would think was a big sacrifice, in truth was an easy choice because I love my work and it kept me away from my family drama and loneliness. So working a lot didn't put me out at all. *So what do I do for others to show them I care? Do I make sacrifices for the people I love? Do I really even love anybody? I love Tabitha. I'd do anything for Tabitha.* I dozed off while the therapist massaged my back.

Chapter 25

WHEN I GOT back to Denver on Saturday, I went straight to the hospital to see Amelia. I was feeling wonderful after a great show, an amazing photo shoot, a long conversation with Tabitha, and just enough time away to stop feeling so much pressure. I was going to stay optimistic that there would be a donor soon and Amelia would survive this, with or without my kidney.

"You look great," I lied. "Much better than you did on Tuesday before I left. Any news?" "Not yet. Hey, Scar, I wanted you to know how much I appreciate you being around. I know how much you hate hospitals. You've been a trooper."

"Well, I…"

"I've put you through a lot, you know, with all the testing and everything to find out if you're a match."

I took a deep breath. My heart started pounding. I had a feeling she knew. "It's okay."

"I don't blame you at all."

"Blame me for what?" I dreaded her saying it.

"For not wanting to give me your kidney."

I sat still. My heart was racing and I was frantically searching for something to say.

"I know you're a match," Amelia said.

Tears welled up and rolled down my cheeks. "I'm sorry," I whispered.

She took a deep breath. "I wasn't sure…"

"I'm sorry." I said again.

"Before you went to New York, you seemed so distant. That's when I figured it out."

"Did somebody tell you?"

"You, right now… But Mom said something, too."

I nodded.

"I'm sorry I'm so sick that I put you in this position."

I couldn't read her. I didn't know what she was trying to say. Is she really going to take responsibility for her life? "I'm sorry you're sick, too."

"You know I love you, right?"

I didn't answer right away.

"Come on, Scarlet, you know how much I love you. I'd do anything for you."

I searched my memory for all the wonderful things she'd done for me over the years to prove her love. Then, I remembered Amelia did do something nice for me once. It was during a week of school when Tabitha was on vacation with her family.

Amelia walked home with me every day that week, so I wouldn't have to walk home alone.

"For the last several months, I didn't care if I lived or died. And I don't blame you for not jumping at the chance to save me. I haven't been a great sister. I know I've put you through a lot. Now, somewhat sober, I can see what I've done, what I've put you and Mom through over the years. I'd like the chance to make it up to you. I'd like the chance to prove to you that I can be better. I'm going to stop the drinking and drugs. I'm going to get my life back. Maybe we could get back on track with the bracelets."

I felt sharp pains in my chest and I didn't want to tell her that I'm too young or that my career is too important. I didn't want to tell her that Mom didn't want me to do it or that Rex didn't want me to do it. Or even that Tabitha didn't think it was right. I didn't know what to say. She was making a plea for her life. I was the judge and the jury and I was handing her a bleak sentence to dialysis until a kidney becomes available for the kidney exchange. "It's complicated, Amelia. You're doing fine on the dialysis. They probably just need to make another adjustment. Mom wants to do the exchange and we should get the news any day…"

"I know. You're right."

Because the guilt was unbearable, I was changing my mind again. I was still distrustful and confused, and I needed to talk to Dr. Windel. "Amelia, I'll be right back." I checked his office but his door was locked. I found paper and a pen in my bag and stuck a note under his door, asking him to call me.

I felt that strong pull from Amelia that I always felt. Tabitha was right, I needed to know the truth about Amelia's situation.

When I went back into her room, I slipped into her bathroom. As I sat on the stool, I got a whiff of a familiar smell and tried to ignore it, convincing myself that it was a hospital smell, probably rubbing alcohol. But just to be sure I pulled the garbage can my way and pulled out some crumpled paper towels. My heart dropped into my stomach when I saw an empty vodka bottle and three miniature Jack Daniel's bottles in the bottom of the garbage can. *It's not possible. It can't be hers. It just can't.*

I grabbed the vodka bottle and marched to the bed. "What's this?"

Amelia's face filled with panic. "What is wrong with you? Why were you digging in the trash? You are such a bitch."

"Who brought it to you?" I demanded.

"None of your business. And I only had a sip," she protested.

"You understand that if you're drinking or drugging, you don't get a kidney, right? And that's not enough to get you to stop?" I shook my head as I stuck the bottle in my bag to hide the evidence. "I can't believe you! You know why you're not getting better on dialysis? Because of this," I said, and pulled the bottle back out.

"Please don't tell. I… I didn't want to. I felt pressure. Please don't tell anyone," Amelia begged while reaching for me.

"Okay!" I started to cry. "I surrender! You have a disease. I'm not mad at you. *I'm not mad at you.* I'm mad at your disease. Amelia," I pleaded. "This disease is going to kill you unless you get stronger than this disease!" I wiped my eyes and took a deep breath. "Dialysis isn't going to work if you're drinking. It will probably make things worse. They most likely won't do a transplant, with me or anybody, if you're drinking. Amelia! You gotta get it together. I don't want to lose you."

When I left Amelia, I searched for Dr. Windel and Dr. Pape, but couldn't find either one. So I called Rex. "Rex," I said, then started sobbing. "Can we get some A.A. people to try to help Amelia?"

"Yeah."

"I don't know what to do," I cried.

"Let me make some phone calls. I'll see what I can round up," Rex said.

Chapter 26

LATER THAT EVENING, I walked into Amelia's room carrying a folding chair, placed it against the wall near the head of her bed and sat down. I was crying. A man came in with his folding chair, set it next to mine and sat down, followed by a woman with her chair. Then another woman followed, then another man. In silence, alcoholics filled Amelia's room. I sat still, crying, because I couldn't believe all these people were doing this for me, for Amelia. Amelia adjusted her bed to sit up straighter and started to cry. We all held hands, and they started with Reinhold Niebuhr's serenity prayer. "God, grant me the serenity to accept the things I cannot change, the courage to change the things I can, and the wisdom to know the difference."

Amelia listened. Every time she looked at me, she cried harder, and then I prayed harder that this would help her.

The opening of the A.A. meeting with Amelia was the same as the first one I had gone to.

"I'm Bob. I'm an alcoholic."

"Hi Bob," we all said in unison.

"Hi, I'm Mary. I'm an alcoholic drug addict."

"Hi, Mary."

"I'm Rex. I'm an alcoholic."

"Hi, Rex."

The group didn't pressure Amelia to say anything, and I didn't introduce myself either. We were both more like spectators.

When it came time to share, they each discussed their struggle with step one: We admitted we were powerless over alcohol—that our lives had become unmanageable.

I continued to silently cry for the entire hour, listening to their stories, how they finally got sober, and how their lives were so much better now. I prayed that Amelia heard what she needed to hear from all these people who had been in her shoes.

Amelia kept wiping her tears as she listened. When the meeting was over, everybody introduced themselves to Amelia and wished her well. They also left her with the twelve steps and a list of everybody's phone number. They encouraged her to call them if she needed anything, even just to talk. When everyone had gone, I held her hands and told her I loved her.

"Thank you." She wiped another tear. "It reminded me of treatment," she said, and smiled. "Thank you for doing that for me."

The entire group was in the parking lot waiting for me. I thanked them all, and they said they would pray for Amelia, then thanked *me* for the opportunity to help a fellow alcoholic. After they left, Rex and I sat in my car and talked. I could tell he was not surprised that Amelia drank. He was almost unaffected by the news.

"And I'm sure she'll drink again," Rex said. "Scarlet, this isn't her choice to quit, people are making her. She doesn't even think she has a problem. In my opinion, she can get a new kidney, get healthy, try to get her life back, but if it's all being forced on her, it won't last. She'll be out drinking again in no time. It's just the nature of the beast."

"Then I don't know what to do."

"Well, I've been thinking. This is entirely your decision, and it will not affect the way I feel about you. I don't have control over you. I wish I did," he said, gently squeezing my leg. "But I know I don't. You make this decision because of how you feel, not because of the way I feel."

"Thank you. I appreciate that."

"I want you to understand that I'd give my kidney to anybody I love who's clean and sober. But I wouldn't give up parts of me for a practicing alcoholic or drug addict. Not a chance. I'd think about it like this… Only do it if you will be okay if she drinks and drugs after recovering from surgery."

"I keep hoping it was a slip, or that the jerk that brought it pressured her. I need to believe she wants a better life?"

"Look, if I had any control over you, like if you were my wife…" He winked at me and smiled. "This would not even be a discussion. I would not let you do it. Maybe I'm a little selfish, but I don't want anything to happen to you. I want to protect you." He tapped on the dash a little. "I don't think your sister is ready to quit, and I can't even believe they'd consider a transplant with somebody who has only been somewhat sober for a few days. I mean, this may not even be up to you, even if you want to do it."

"That's what Tabitha said, too. I tried to find Dr. Windel today to talk to him about Amelia but, I doubt he'd tell me anything because of that HIPAA."

"Maybe that counselor could tell you something. Didn't Amelia sign a release?"

"Yes, I tried to find her, too." I stared ahead and clutched the steering wheel. "I just want this to be her bottom. She drinks and I'm devastated. Why isn't she devastated? I don't think this is her bottom… Seriously, Rex, shouldn't this be her bottom?"

"For too many, their bottom is death. It's the only way they quit. But you might want to try to figure out why you like having an alcoholic sister."

"I don't. She has been nothing but a heartache for me."

"Yes, but you have always been there for her. You've never left her, so what are you getting out of it?"

"That's stupid. I've always wanted a healthy, happy sister. I did everything to try to help her get to that…"

"No, there's more to it. What would your life be like if your sister was healthy?"

"It would be wonderful. We'd have a lot of fun together."

"What if she's too busy for you, going to A.A. meetings and hanging out with A.A. people? What if having her sick, in some ways, kept her close to you and your mother? What if she gets healthy, and she doesn't want to spend a lot of time with you? What if she gets married and has kids and spends time with other couples with kids? Is that the sister you want?"

"Yes, it is. We've never been close. I've always wanted to be close with her, but you can't get close to an alcoholic. I think I have a better chance of a relationship with her if she's sober. I just want her happy. I don't want to have to worry about her anymore."

"You're never together, but you're always there to rescue her. So in some ways, you're always connected to her, very attached in many ways. Maybe co-dependent, because why else would you hide the bottle."

"I don't want her to die!" I raised my voice. "If I tell them, there's no chance she'll get the kidney... I'd feel even more guilt." I looked at him "Do you know anything about dialysis?"

"No, I don't. Why?"

"In the back of my mind, I mean, if she could live on dialysis, which I think some people can, at least she'd have to show up and she'd probably have to take better care of herself. She'd have to check in with nurses, so she couldn't be drunk. She'd have to be accountable. I think she'd have to get her life right. There would be other people keeping an eye on her, not just me and Mom. We'd have help."

"Let me ask you this, Scarlet. If Amelia gets a kidney, gets clean and sober and is well, then what will you do with your life? You'll no longer have to rescue her or be on call for her."

"It'd be like heaven," I said, exhaling, as if releasing all my stress. "I'd feel free. But it's hard to imagine, because I've been living like this for so long." I paused to think about what that might be like. "I'd focus on my career and make plans for my future... I used to live in New York, but then, always feeling needed here, I sold my condo and moved back to Denver. I'd spend more time with Tabitha, maybe I'd be in a relationship, maybe I'd start a side business. I'd keep busy, and try to have a better relationship with my mom…"

"Maybe you should start doing all of that now. Maybe you should have been doing that all along and having Amelia sick gave you a reason or excuse not to do those other things. Those are the things that scare you the most, being in a relationship, starting a side business, having a better relationship with your mom. Maybe Amelia's troubles keep you safe in some way."

I felt stupid. Rex was right. Why don't I live my life the way I want? What's holding me back? "You might be onto something, Rex. I honestly don't know what I'm going to do after modeling, and I am really scared about losing my career with nothing to fall back on. I've never been in a relationship, and I sometimes blamed Amelia for that. I blame her for my distant relationship with my mom, too."

"Maybe we could work on that relationship part right away," Rex said, and smiled.

Butterflies filled my stomach and I smiled back, hoping he was serious.

"Scarlet, I know we haven't known each other very long, but there is nobody else I'd rather be with. I want to be in a committed relationship with you."

I couldn't believe this was happening. I couldn't stop smiling, but instead of saying *Yes, I want the same thing*, I said, "Why?"

He smiled and sat up a little straighter. "Well, there are a few reasons. I'm incredibly attracted to you. I think you're funny, and I love your sense of humor. I actually got a kick out of your lively spirit the first day I met you, and I know that part of you doesn't come out often, probably mainly when you're stressed and struggling with some hard issues. So, basically, I

believe this is a gift most men would wish for. I will always
know that when you get gutsy mad about something, it's time to
talk. It's like having my own little warning button that goes off,
it's time to nurture Scarlet and find out what is wrong. That's a
little trick I have up my sleeve." He winked at me. "Besides that,
I love that you love your work. I love that you keep busy. I love
that you have a life outside of me, because I'm also a busy person with dreams and goals. I know you like me, but you don't
call me that often, you don't share every detail about your life. I
find you mysterious in a way that's refreshing. I feel we have a
connection. Sadly, some of it's because of alcoholism and addiction, but I think you understand the beast and you probably
have a good idea of my struggles. I just think we would make a
good team in life," he said.

"Okay, you've convinced me. I'd like to be in a relationship
with you, too. I'm in."

"Why?"

I giggled. "Well, you don't pressure me. You don't try to
control me, other than with Amelia, but I like your concern. I
like that you want to protect me. I like your sense of humor,
and I especially think it's funny that you think I'm funny. I don't
think I'm funny, but I'd like to be funny." I looked straight
ahead and said, "And then ditto on everything else you said."

"See, that's funny." He gave me a little nudge. "Okay,
what's next? Maybe we should call your mom so you can spend
some time with her."

"One at a time, Rex. And you have to understand that I
don't really like to be around her. I don't know what type of
relationship we have or what hope we have. When I was at her
place helping her paint the wall, I felt so distant and sad. I

wanted to try to get close to her, but I couldn't. Then the other day, she really came through for me. You have no idea how much that meant to me… She seems to flip-flop a lot. Just when I think we are going to start getting close, she turns on me and everything goes back to the way it was."

That night in bed, I couldn't decide what Amelia offered me as a sick sister. What did I gain by having a sick sister? Did I help keep her sick? I knew Mom did, but did I? Or was this all just part of the process of having an addict in the family? Could I help her? Was there anything I could do that would make a difference? I'd enabled her and I'd walked away from her. Nothing had made a difference. I hated feeling helpless. Having a sick sister gave me a maddening distraction, and many excuses for why I didn't really have a life of my own. I didn't have a boyfriend. I had a career dictated by others, and I was afraid to branch out and do something for myself. Having a sick sister kept me in a place that was comfortable, familiar.

Chapter 27

WHEN I WENT to see Amelia the next morning, I decided not to say anything about the bottle to Amelia's doctors, but I wasn't going to let Amelia forget that I knew about her lack of concern for me, Mom, and herself. If it was just a slip, nobody needed to know. I didn't need to take her inventory. If she was on track, she would tell Dr. Pape herself, so I'd wait and see if she came clean.

When I was almost to Amelia's room, I saw her in the hall, in a wheelchair, heading down for dialysis. She asked me to go with her. I didn't want to, but I did. I couldn't believe what she was going through. The nurse gave her a couple of shots and then he stuck a large needle into her. I felt like I was going to be sick or pass out. I couldn't stand to watch and Amelia's flirting with the nurse didn't even distract me enough. I had to get out of there.

While I waited for more than an hour in Amelia's room, I used my phone to Google how to find the prefect career, how to market jewelry and bracelets, and how to patch up mother-daughter relationships. When Amelia got back, she looked pale. The nurse told her he would adjust the speed of the fluids next time and she should do much better. "I think we're going to have to stick with the daily instead of every other day, Amelia. Don't worry, we'll get it figured out. We're in the adjustment period," he said as he helped her into bed. "You take it easy, okay?" He nodded to me as he left the room.

"You okay?" I asked her.

"Not really. I'm cramping, feel like I'm going to throw up."

I moved the trash can closer to her bed. "I'll go get you some water."

When I got back with the water, Amelia was sleeping so I set the water by her bed and left. I was disappointed; I had wanted to spend the day with her because I was going out of town again for a Gucci shoot in Miami.

When I stepped into the elevator, Dr. Pape was also going down. "I'm going to the cafeteria. You want to join me?" she asked.

"Sure."

I got a bottle of water while she got a cup of coffee, and we sat down at a table. "How are you doing?" she asked.

"I guess I'm just sad, because I've made a lot of mistakes. I've enabled Amelia to get this bad."

"That's what we do when we love somebody. We try to help them, but it turns out we're hurting them. I lost my sister to addiction."

"I didn't know," I said, putting my hand over my heart. "I'm so sorry."

"It's okay. It was years ago. That's why I got into this profession. I wanted to help other families avoid the mistakes my parents and I made. Unfortunately, most don't reach out to me until it's very late in the game. Amelia is late in the game."

"I know. I keep racking my brain trying to figure out where this all went wrong. I even think back to when we were kids. I remember that whenever we went to a restaurant, Amelia was outgoing and wanted to be the center of attention. She always got the extra care from the host and servers. They'd say how cute she was or what a great little personality she had. But if, for some reason, she didn't get enough attention, it never failed that Amelia would spill her milk or cry about her food not being what she wanted. She's been like that for as long as I can remember."

"It's funny what we remember about our childhoods."

"It just makes me wonder how I could have helped her so it didn't get to this point. I've been going to Al-Anon meetings and I'm starting to really understand how much I enabled her. I've taken care of all her bills. I've paid her rent. I let her live with me or she's lived with Mom. She's never had much responsibility. I, on the other hand, have always been responsible. I take care of Amelia, Mom, and myself." I shook my head. "I wanted to make their lives easier. I was proud I could help them, but now that pride is turning into frustration."

"You're a good sister, and I pray it isn't too late to save Amelia's life. She's very sick, physically and psychologically. I've told her how sick she is, but sadly she doesn't believe me and she doesn't seem to care. Even after detox, that pull for alcohol is very strong, especially because of the stress she's under. This disease has taken everything from her. Vodka has been her family and friends and her doctor and counselor over the years."

"And prescriptions. You know, her back has bothered her for a long time."

"Yes, probably just as long as she's been drinking heavily. We believe her back pain might have actually been kidney pain."

"Seriously?" I was dumbfounded. I couldn't believe it.

"That's what we're thinking. The only chance she has is if she can stay sober."

"She was in rehab once, maybe twice."

"Yes, she told me."

"That's a good sign, right?"

"Scarlet, I'm not going to sugar coat this. Amelia has a tough road ahead of her, and so do you."

"I know," I said, and looked down. "I think I'm going to do the surgery…"

Dr. Pape raised her eyebrows and looked shocked. "I think you'd better talk to Dr. Windel." Just then her beeper went off. She looked at it, then said, "I have to get going. Thanks for joining me for coffee… and water." She gently tapped my forearm, then hurried off to the elevators.

Chapter 28

WHEN I GOT back from Miami, I went straight to the hospital to check on Amelia. I expected her to start feeling and looking better, but when I got there she was sleeping and she looked awful. Her skin looked greenish, and she was puffy.

I found Dr. Windel and Dr. Pape talking in the hall. "Why isn't Amelia getting better?" I demanded. "She's off all the pain pills. She's on dialysis. She should be getting better. I read that people live on dialysis for years. You could live your whole life on dialysis."

"It's not that simple, Scarlet. A lot of damage has been done," Dr. Pape said.

"But why isn't everything starting to heal? It seems like she's getting worse, not better. And why haven't we found the donor for the exchange? My mom is ready for the surgery."

"Amelia isn't stable. We need to be sure she can handle the surgery," Dr. Windel said.

Dr. Pape gave him a look of disappointment.

"Is there anything I can do? Can I take her home for a while? Maybe that would lift her spirits."

"Scarlet, honey," Dr. Pape said. "You know patients that continue to abuse are not candidates for transplant."

"What? What do you mean? She wants her life back. She's done drinking."

"I caught her with a bottle this morning," Dr. Pape said, and gave me a defeated look.

I started crying. "No! She wouldn't do that!"

Both Dr. Pape and Dr. Windel nodded their heads. I turned around and ran back to Amelia's room. "Amelia. Amelia," I cried, and shook her to wake her up.

"Hi Scar. What's wrong?"

"Amelia, are you still drinking? Dr. Pape said you were drinking," I cried.

"No, Scar. I wouldn't do…"

"Then why do they think you are?" I shook her some more. "Amelia, you don't get it!

This is life or death! You're going to die if you don't stop! Do you understand? You have to get better before you can get the transplant. They don't think you're strong enough. Are you eating?"

"I can't eat. I'm tired, Scar. Let's talk in the morn…"

She fell back asleep, and I couldn't wake her.

I left the hospital and called Mom to see if I could stop by. She said she was going to bed early and she'd talk to me in the morning. She seemed mad at me again. *What else is new?*

I didn't sleep at all that night. I kept thinking that if I had just said yes and given Amelia my kidney while she still had strength, before they knew she was still drinking, then maybe she'd be doing okay. Or at least better than she was now.

After several hours of tossing and turning, the phone rang. "Honey," Mom sobbed, "Amelia passed away… she's gone."

I didn't say anything, I didn't believe her. I started to cry.

"Scarlet… Amelia's gone."

Chapter 29

AFTER THE FUNERAL, I wouldn't leave the cemetery. Even after the guys came to finish burying the casket, I stayed. I sat on a bench under a tree, several tombstones away from Amelia. All the leaves were off the trees, and winter was moving in. I couldn't believe she was gone. I couldn't believe everything I had with her was over. Now what? Now what was I supposed to do?

Rex had gone back to the church with the others to celebrate Amelia's life over coffee and cookies, so I was left alone to grieve. After about an hour and a half, I noticed Rex had come back and parked on the street outside of the cemetery. He got out of his truck and walked toward me, but before he got too close he asked, "Can I join you?"

I nodded, so he sat down next to me. I was glad he didn't say anything. I expected he'd say the usual things that most people say like, "How are you doing?" or, "I know how you're feeling." And how do you answer back when all you really want to say is, "How do you think I'm doing?" or "How could you possibly know how I feel?" In truth, I just wanted to tell almost everybody to fuck off. But I wanted Rex and Tabitha to stay close.

We sat in silence and I started to cry again. He wrapped his arm over my shoulder and pulled me against him, and I burrowed my head into his chest. I was in so much pain. I didn't know how I could live with so much pain. "I couldn't save her from the addiction, but when I had the chance to save her life, I chose not to. How am I going to live with myself?"

He gave me a little squeeze, but said nothing.

"My chest aches. I feel like I'm going to die from the pain in my heart," I said, trying to fight the tears. "How can I go on living? I let her down. I feel like I killed her, like I killed my sister."

"Scarlet, she was already dead inside, and now she's no longer in pain. Now that she's free, she would never want you hurting like this. She wants everything for you that you wanted for her."

It sounded good, and I wanted to believe it.

"Scarlet, you have to grieve, and it's going to suck. But you have to know that this whole thing was not your fault. It really had nothing to do with you."

For almost two hours Rex stayed with me. It was getting dark and cold, and I was ready to go home. I wanted to stay with her, but I knew I couldn't stay there forever.

~~~~

I spent the next week home alone, crying. Rex stopped by occasionally to bring me food and talk, but no one called, not even Tabitha. That surprised me, but I was too sad to wonder why. I hadn't talked to her since the funeral. I called Mom a couple times, but she was as depressed as I was and didn't want to talk.

When I was finally showering and moving around, I tried to call Tabitha, but she didn't answer. I was starting to get concerned, so I kept calling, even though I knew her heavy workload and her new boyfriend were probably taking up all her time. Pete was with her at the funeral, and barely acknowledged me. I tried to give him the benefit of the doubt and figured he was shy or uncomfortable being at a funeral for somebody he didn't know. I figured he was part of the reason Tabitha and I didn't talk much that day; she had seemed distant and annoyed, but I was glad Pete was there for her.

That night I had a horrible dream that Tabitha called me. She was headed back to town to see her parents and wanted to meet with me. I was in a bad place, so meeting her for lunch gave me something to look forward to. I really needed her. The plan was to have our lunch and then Rex was going to join us for coffee and dessert, so he could get to know her better. They didn't really get the chance to talk at the funeral.

Tabitha was already at the restaurant when I got there. She seemed mad at me, cold.

"Hey, Tab. Am I late?" I asked as I checked the time on my phone. I was ten minutes early.

"I got here a little early. I need to talk to you." She closed her menu. "Scarlet, I will always love you and you will always hold a special place in my heart, but I can no longer be your friend."

"What do you mean?" I gasped.

"I'm a doctor, Scarlet. I'm all about saving lives, and you were too worried about your career to save your sister's life."

"That's not true, Tabitha. It was more than that. You know our history. You know her history…"

"It doesn't matter. You're a different person than I thought you were. And I can't have a friend who is so careless with the people who should mean everything."

"I'm in shock right now." I shook my head, desperately trying to find the words to fix this, and I started to cry. "I don't know what to say, other than I love you, I'll always love you. You have been the most important person in my life." I reached for her hand, but she pulled away. "I would have done it for you…"

"No, you wouldn't, not if it would ruin your precious career."

"Tabitha, it wasn't about that. Come on! You know me. You know me. I'm not the person you're saying I am. Tabitha…" I pleaded.

"I'm sorry, I have to go. I truly hope you have a good life. And I hope you are never left waiting for somebody you love to come through for you."

All of my pain and guilt flooded back over me and I lowered my head to the table and cried as she walked out.

~~~~

"Scarlet. Scarlet, wake up."

I woke up sobbing. Rex was lying next to me on my bed, and he held me as I told him about my dream. My stomach ached and my heart felt hollow in my chest. "What if she doesn't want to be in my life anymore? I can't get ahold of her. What if this is true? What if she feels this way about me?" I cried.

"I can't believe she's not calling you back, especially right now. She must be going through something herself. Was she close to Amelia? I don't think she understands the complexity of Amelia's situation. Can I call her?"

"No," I said. "And I'm going to stop calling her, too. I've left messages." I felt the tears run down my temples and into my hair. I could tell my lips were swelling and my eyes were red. I was thankful I didn't have a job lined up. I felt alone without my best friend and I was scared. I was afraid that I was wrong about Tabitha, that maybe she wasn't the friend I thought. I was afraid that she was turning away from me. And although it was a dream, it felt so real. How could my very best friend for life so easily walk away from me?

After repeatedly telling Rex what a great friend Tabitha was to me, I was starting to feel foolish. I felt like he would start thinking less of me, too. All I ever talked about was how great Tabitha was—the greatest person in the world, the best friend anybody could have, nobody in the world better than her—and then have her avoid me. Now I was questioning everything about my relationships. I felt very alone. My throat was swollen and my heart was heavy with regret. My eyes were burning and my head was pounding with pressure. How did all of this happen?

Tabitha was the one person who always made me feel like everything would be okay. But without her usual supportive, encouraging talks, I was starting to feel another major loss in my life. It didn't change the way I felt about her. She would always be my best friend, and if she ever needed me, I'd be there for her.

"Scarlet, it's good you're grieving, you should. But you need to pick a date when you want to get on with your life. Maybe when you're ready to get back to work. You love what you do, so that will cheer you up," Rex said.

"You're right. I will."

"And about Tabitha, I wouldn't give her another thought. Maybe she's been a good friend in the past, but she isn't right now. I sure hope she comes around because you deserve better friends. I hope she calls you tomorrow and proves she's still the good friend she's always been."

He lay there on the bed with me with his hand resting on my stomach, while I wept over the loss of my sister and the possibility that I'd lost my best friend.

Chapter 30

I TRIED HARD to pull myself together and I even made plans to get back to work. My life was totally different now. I had my first boyfriend, but my sister was gone and Tabitha, it seemed, was gone, too. She didn't return my calls and I stopped calling. My mom was more distant with every passing day. Not having really talked to her since Amelia's funeral, I decided to go to her place to check on her. I rang the bell and waited.

She answered the door, but didn't say anything. I could tell she had been crying. I followed her to the living room and I sat down on the couch.

"Would you like some coffee?" she asked as she walked toward the kitchen.

"Sure. How are you doing, Mom?"

In that instant, she turned and came charging back at me, shaking her finger in my face and scolding me. "You were so mean to her. You had no sympathy for what she was going through. You are selfish and self-centered. She'd be alive right now if you had given... You! You killed her!"

I sat there trying to catch my breath with tears welling up in my eyes. I'd never seen her so hysterical.

"I don't care if I ever see you again. I don't want a daughter like you. How could you let her die? How could you let her die?" she sobbed, as she fell to the floor.

I said nothing through my tears and got up to leave. I didn't bother trying to comfort her. As I walked by the kitchen, I saw a few prescription bottles on the counter.

Everything she had said to me, I already believed about myself. I felt responsible for Amelia, and I let everybody down. In my heart, I wanted to believe I was a good person but it seemed Tabitha no longer wanted to be in my life. Amelia had told me I was selfish and self-centered and now, Mom, who has said the same thing most of my adult life, is repeating it to me. Everybody I love is reflecting my feelings about who I am, how I feel, and what I deserve.

I cried as I drove to an Al-Anon meeting. I wanted to be around other people suffering from heartache but who wouldn't blame me or attack me. I sat though the meeting, crying with a wad of tissue in my hand to dry my eyes. Two women spoke about losing their children to addiction. One had a daughter who was an alcoholic who often got behind the wheel of her car. "One night it was raining, she was drunk, and she ran off a bridge. Some wanted to believe it was suicide, but my baby was pregnant. If she had known she was pregnant, she would have stopped drinking. And there's no way she would have killed herself."

The other woman's son was addicted to heroin. He overdosed or mixed it with something and slipped into a coma. After two months the family decided to stop life support, and he died shortly after. "My whole life has fallen apart since we lost him. I just don't know how to live anymore. I think about him every minute of every day."

It didn't look like either of the women had recovered yet. I thought it was strange how I ended up at that meeting and heard the things I heard. I needed to hear the pain from these mothers. In that instant, I forgave my mom for the things she had said to me.

Chapter 31

THE NEXT DAY I decided to go and spend some time with Amelia. I was thankful nobody was at the cemetery. I wanted to be alone with her. After looking at all the other decorated graves, I was sorry that I hadn't brought flowers. I found her tombstone and sat down next to her to talk. It was real again that she was gone. "I'm so sorry I couldn't save you. I loved you so much. Even though I was frustrated with you, I never stopped loving you. I'll always love you."

The wind picked up and the leaves started dancing around. I pulled my coat a little tighter around my neck. "I wish you were here with me right now. I'm a mess. I don't think anybody can help me, and I don't even know if I can help myself. I've lost everybody. You, Tabitha, Mom. I don't know what I'm going to do. I wish I could go back in time. I wish I had done things differently. I wasn't a good sister to you. I tried, but everything I did was wrong. Everything."

I lay down on the brown grass and looked to the gray sky. I reached up to stop a tear and closed my eyes. I wanted to connect with Amelia or God or somebody who could make everything okay. I wanted so badly for everything to be okay.

It felt like somebody was watching me, so I slowly opened my eyes, and startled, I sat up. There, sitting right next to me, was a gray and white cat. "Oh, you scared me!" I said as I slowly reached over and petted her. She meowed.

"What are you doing here?" I asked the cat. She came a little closer and rubbed up against my side. Then she lunged at me to rub against my arm, then my back. I giggled. I'd never seen a cat lunge like that. She kept doing it, rearing up and then lunging to rub against me. I kept petting her as she loudly purred, and I started to cry again. I thought about Mystic.

Then she bit my bracelet. "No, no, honey, you can't have that," I said and looked at the bracelet to make sure it wasn't damaged. She reared up and lunged at me, almost head butting me, then rubbed against my shoulder. She went after my bracelet again, her whiskers and cool nose tickling my wrist. "No, baby, no," I giggled. I checked the bracelet once more, then pulled my legs up and hugged them as I examined the leather.

The cat kept lunging and rubbing against me as I looked closely at Amelia's bracelet. I remembered the promise I had made to myself—I wouldn't take the bracelet off until Amelia was clean and sober. A part of me didn't want to be without it, because the bracelet kept me close to her, but Amelia's drinking days were over, and I prayed she was happy and healthy and no longer in pain.

I unhooked the bracelet's clasp and rolled over to my stomach. The cat was frantically grabbing at the bracelet, then crawling across my back, making me smile. Using my car key and my fingers, I dug a little hole by the drying plants, and I buried Amelia's bracelet.

Chapter 32

I CONTINUED GOING to the Al-Anon meetings and occasionally to the A.A. meetings. They were a place to go where people didn't judge me, because most of the people there had made bad decisions, too. It made me feel human, imperfect and deserving of forgiveness. Besides Rex, they were the only people I told the truth to about how Amelia had kept drinking when she was in the hospital.

Marge, an older woman in the Al-Anon group, continually told me I did the right thing. "She would have ruined your kidney, too, honey. She wasn't going to quit drinking and drugging," she said in a motherly tone.

It was nice to hear, but I'd never know that, because I never gave Amelia the chance.

Another woman basically said the same thing, "I don't believe her. As soon as she was feeling a little better, she'd be right back out there. They are so manipulative, especially when they want something."

I liked their brutal honesty, but sometimes their attacks against Amelia stung even though I knew they were just trying to comfort me. I didn't talk much, but when I did, I became very aware that if I was going to talk about my experiences and be honest about my life, I was going to get feedback and it might not always be the feedback I wanted. In fact, it was almost never the feedback I was looking for.

After every Al-Anon meeting, Marge hugged me and said, "Now you get out there and live a life good enough for two, for the both of you. Make her proud." That always choked me up. I loved Marge, and she was starting to be a very good friend to me. We had even met for coffee a couple of times. She was happily married to her second husband, with two cats but no kids. She was happy and smart, and I loved talking to her.

One night after a meeting, I was going to Rex's for dinner because I was off to New York the next day for a runway. I was really looking forward to getting back to work. I got to Rex's place just as the Chinese restaurant delivery guy was leaving. Perfect, I thought, as I was craving Chinese and I figured it was light enough before a big show.

"How you holding up?" he asked, then gave me a hug.

"I'm doing okay as long as I'm not thinking about Amelia, Tabitha, or my mom. Which is almost never."

"Well, why don't you sit down and relax. I'll serve you," he said, then took my coat and led me to the table.

I sat down and watched Rex get the glasses of water, plates and silverware. "Are you sure you don't want help?"

"I'm sure." He placed a plate in front of me then handed me a couple boxes to choose from.

"Mmm. Moo Goo Gai Pan. Thank you for having me over for dinner. This is wonderful."

"I'm trying to make things equal, since I spend a lot of time at your place."

"Yes, and it's nice to have a little change of scenery for me. Sometimes I think my walls are closing in on me."

"Your mom will come around," he said, reaching for the carton of fried rice. "I don't understand that Tabitha thing, but I have a feeling she's going to miss you and come around, too."

"I don't know," I said, and took a drink of water. "I think I'm doing better than I thought I would. I'm still devastated by everything, but I'm starting to function. I hope I'm not moving too fast."

"I just can't imagine what you're going through. I think that's why I don't get too close to people these days. It keeps me safe."

I felt like I had been kicked in the chest. What did he mean, he doesn't get close to people? Isn't that what we'd been doing the last several weeks, getting close to each other? "I guess I don't know what you mean. You seem close to a lot of people."

"You were so close to Tabitha and look how bad she was able to hurt you. I think you just loved her too much. You didn't protect yourself. That's why she was able to hurt you."

What he was saying wasn't getting any better, it was getting worse. "You can't be serious. I mean, don't we all long for close relationships?"

"Of course, but people can be jerks. I'm just saying it's good to stay somewhat protected. If you don't care that much, you don't get hurt."

My heart started aching. "I don't regret my friendship with Tabitha. I regret a lot of things in my life, but I don't regret loving Tabitha the way I do. I don't regret loving anyone. I'm glad I'm capable of that kind of love." I had wondered if Rex thought less of me because Tabitha didn't seem to love me the same way I loved her. Well, I guess I had my answer. He thought I was foolish. He thought he was getting to know a strong woman, but now he was looking at me as if I was weak, vulnerable, stupid. "You don't have to worry about me, I'm fine. I'll be fine," I said.

"I know you will. You're strong."

No I'm not! I was panicking inside. What was he trying to say? Was he getting ready to leave me, too? I took a deep breath, and decided he was warning me not to get close to him. He was telling me that he'd never be close to me. He was never going to love me, the way I wanted to love him. He won't love me the way I need to be loved. What is the point to any of this? My stomach became knotted and I lost my appetite. "I'm sorry, I guess I wasn't as hungry as I thought." *Oh God, please don't break up with me. Please don't break up with me.* I started to cry.

"What's wrong? Are you okay?"

"I don't know. I guess I'm… Maybe I'm tired."

"Well, let's go sit in the living room, and I'll clean this up later. Come on." He helped me up. "Maybe you shouldn't be alone tonight. Why don't you stay with me?"

"Thanks, but I can't. I have to get up early, so maybe I should go home and go to bed."

"Do you want me to drive you? I can drive your car then take a cab back. It's no problem."

"No, it's okay. I'm okay."

"Will you call me when you get home so I know you made it safely?"

"Sure. I'm sorry about this. Thanks for dinner," I said.

"Let me pack some up for you."

"No. I probably won't eat before I leave town, and it'll go to waste." I rushed out the door, saying, "Thanks. Good night," over my shoulder.

"Call me when you get home," he yelled. "I don't want to worry about you."

I cried all the way home, believing Rex didn't care that much about me and that maybe he was going to break up with me. I lay awake all night thinking about being without Amelia, without my mother, without Tabitha and now without Rex.

Chapter 33

NEW YORK WASN'T my best show ever, but I survived getting back to work. While I was there, Mae called me and told me that Gucci wanted me back in Miami for another shoot. She was thrilled, and so was I. I had to keep working, but now that I *was* back to work, something had shifted and I didn't know if I felt the same love for my career as I had before. Everything in my world seemed different.

I was also worried about my relationship with Rex; another reason New York hadn't gone so great. I couldn't stop thinking about him. I was in love with him, and I was afraid of losing him. I wondered if it was time we became more physical. I wanted to make out with him, but I was scared. Maybe it was time. What do I have to lose? Maybe it would stop him from pulling away from me. Maybe we'd get closer.

When I got home from the airport, I called Rex and invited him over. When he got to my place we sat down on the couch, and in my desperate attempt to hold on to him, I kissed him. And as if by my one kiss, I unleashed his passion. He became aroused and his hands eagerly explored my body. I couldn't breathe. His touch felt amazing and frightening at the same time. I couldn't stop him. I didn't want to stop him. I didn't want to lose him. I wanted to be taken out of my pain. I wanted to forget everything. I wanted somebody to want me. I wanted somebody to love me.

Everything happened so fast, and my cries of pain seemed to push him harder. Blood covered the couch, and his penis, and when Rex saw the blood, he panicked. "What is this?" he had blood on his hand. "Are you a virgin? Oh my God! Why didn't you tell me? God, Scarlet, I'm so sorry. I didn't know."

I sat on the couch in tears, not knowing if I was crying because of Amelia or Tabitha or the tearing pain between my legs or if I was crying over the loss of my virginity. Rex put his arms around me, drawing me to him, and started to cry. "Scarlet, I am so sorry. Oh my God! What did I just do? Oh my God. Come with me." He reached for my hand and helped me up. I was dazed. I couldn't believe what had just happened. I couldn't believe I was no longer a virgin. I wasn't mad at Rex, but I didn't know how I felt. My thoughts were muddled. I was still bleeding.

He led me into the bathroom and started the shower. "I fucked up. I really fucked up. I shouldn't have been so rough with you. Your first time should have been… Please forgive me, Scarlet. Please forgive me. I'm going to make this up to you. I'll make it up to you. Fuck! Scarlet, why didn't you tell me? I hurt you, didn't I? I'm sorry." He helped me into the shower and joined me. He stopped talking, but kept holding on to me and the water washed away the blood. I didn't understand anything that he was saying. I felt numb. I just didn't care. The tears kept coming but I couldn't talk. I couldn't say anything.

"I'm going to make this up to you. Please, you have to let me make this up to you. It's not how it should have been. You know that, right? I made a mistake. Not your mistake, mine. I'm going to fix it. I just never would have thought..." He got out of the shower and told me to take my time. "We'll have dinner tonight. I'm going to make this up to you, you'll see."

When I was finished drying off, I wrapped the towel around me and walked down the hall. I heard Rex on the phone talking, and I stopped and listened. "I'm crazy about this girl," he said, "but I fucked up. She lost her sister, her best friend and now I just... I don't want to fuck this up, but I think I already did." I stepped into the room and Rex saw me. "I gotta go. Yes, I'll get to a meeting. Thanks man."

"Scarlet, that was my sponsor. He's my best friend. I feel so bad and I needed to talk to him. I don't know what to do right now, but I know I want to be with you. I want to continue our relationship if that's okay with you. I never would have done this, like this, if I had known you hadn't been with anybody before. I would have wanted to make your first time a good experience for you. I feel like I blew it. I really hope I didn't screw this up."

As I listened to him, I realized that I didn't have anybody to talk to. Tabitha was gone, Amelia was gone, and I'd never talk to Mom about something like this. My modeling friends would laugh at me for still being a virgin. The weight of not having

Tabitha and Amelia grew heavier. I had nobody to talk to about my first time.

Chapter 34

MAE CALLED ME the next morning and wanted me to go to Europe for a week. Still in shock about what had happened the night before, I was anxious to get away from everything, especially Rex. I needed some space to let it all sink in, but before I caught my flight, I did text him to tell him I was going out of town.

I decided to try to get back to the one thing that always made me feel good about myself and my life. And if things didn't work out with Rex, maybe moving back to New York wasn't such a bad idea. As long as I had my career, I would survive all the pain and remorse I felt for all of my mistakes. Leaving my past in Denver seemed like a good idea.

Since the time I left Dubai, it had been a long, hard couple of months, with only small modeling jobs along the way. Though still sorting through my emotions, I was eagerly ready to get back to modeling. Sitting in the makeup chair again felt incredible, until the makeup artist commented about the dark puffiness under my eyes. "Scarlet, we gotta do something about those eyes. What've you been doin', girl?" She giggled.

I was taken aback, I hadn't been *doin'* anything and I didn't see the problem. I thought I looked the same as I'd always looked. It put me in a bad mood. I had never been put down like that before, especially by a makeup artist. "I... I don't know," I said, and looked in the mirror. I couldn't see any puffiness or dark circles under my eyes, so I said, "I don't know what you mean."

"Never mind. I'll do my best with what I have to work with, and they can fix the eyes after the shoot. They'll touch 'em up. It'll be fine," she said, and giggled again.

I was ready, but they were still making some adjustments on the set, so I called Mae, who seemed too busy for me. "Mae, I'm never working with this girl from makeup again. She doesn't know what she's doing and she's rude."

"Oh, I see. You take a break from modeling and now you're a diva! I told you a long time ago, you have to show up. You know, we didn't leave you, you left us. I don't have time for this," she said, and hung up on me.

"I wasn't taking a break," I said. "Hello? Hello?" I wanted to cry, but I put my phone back with my things and told myself to settle down before they called me over. *I can do this. I'm fine. My eyes are fine. I'm not a diva.*

"You look great, Scarlet. We are so happy to have you back. We've all really missed you."

That's more like it. I was suddenly back and happy to be back. I took position, took a deep breath and took direction while listening to my favorite sound of the clicking camera.

"Come on, Scarlet, connect. Connect. Connect."

What is he talking about? I am connecting. What is going on?

"Scarlet, honey, relax your forehead, relax your eyes. You're looking a little heavy on your face. Relax."

I heard them whispering about me. I couldn't figure out what I was doing wrong. Maybe the stress of everything in my life was catching up to me, maybe I needed counseling. "Just tell me what to do and I'll do it," I said.

"We've been telling you. You need to relax. We're not getting the shot, Scarlet."

This had never happened to me before. I was so discouraged I wanted to cry. I tried different tricks I'd learned over the years. *Modeling is acting, so act.* I acted like I hadn't a care in the world. I acted like I was happy. I acted like I was very light and relaxed. *Always face the light. You can't go wrong if you face the light.* I made sure I was facing the light. Getting in, getting the shot, and getting out was key, but this shoot had been the longest I'd been on. I couldn't connect, and they couldn't get the shot.

"All right, Scarlet, this was a tough one. We're done. I hope we got it."

I started crying instantly after they said we were done. "I'm sorry, I don't know what's wrong with me."

"I know you've been through a lot. I'm really hoping we got something to work with," he said, setting his camera down. "We're rooting for you, Scarlet, but you gotta find a way to relax."

"I will, I promise. I'll do better." I walked back to makeup to change. I'd never been as scared about my career or my future as I was in that moment.

~~~~

I had another shoot the next day with a different photographer and it happened all over again. "Your face. Your face. Your face. Scarlet, relax your face!"

I took a few deep breaths to release the tension then tried again.

"Where's your energy? We need energy."

Then I heard one of the guys say, "She's photographing old."

"Well, she might have hit her prime," the photographer said.

I felt panic and desperation and said, "I have to go to the bathroom."

"Great," the photographer said sarcastically.

I went back to makeup and saw Emily, another model. "Emily, do you have something to help me relax?"

She smiled broadly and said, "Of course, Scarlet. Most girls like oxy," she said and handed me a pill from a prescription bottle.

"Thanks," I said, as I stepped to the mini fridge and grabbed a bottle of water. I snapped the pill in half, swallowed one piece and stuck the other half in my bra.

After a few minutes I felt a little fuzzy, but it was just enough to get me over the hump. I was pretty sure the guys got the shot even though I was trouble on the set. I had to figure this out so I could get my career back on track.

Later that night Emily called me and asked if I wanted to go out. She knew I was having trouble and wanted to help take my mind off things.

"That sounds great. I'd love to."

"Great. We'll probably hook up with a few other girls. I'll meet you in the lobby in twenty minutes?"

"Prefect. See you then." I was a little nervous because I knew her reputation, but she did help me out, and I could use a distraction. We walked to a nightclub just a couple blocks from the hotel and met up with three other models, all younger than me. I was flattered that they knew who I was. When it was time to order drinks, I ordered a diet coke. I didn't want to mix alcohol with the drug I had taken at the shoot. The other girls ordered drinks with alcohol, and I noticed some pills being handed out. I asked for a pill, too. "Is it oxy?"

"Sure thing. You liked it, huh?" she said, handing me two pills.

"It took the edge off. Thanks for helping me out." I pretended to take the pills, but I slipped them into my pocket to save for later. I actually wanted them in case I had more trouble with the photographers.

"You're welcome. No drinking?"

"No, it doesn't agree with me."

"Maybe you've been drinking the wrong thing," she said.

"Not tonight. Maybe another night. Is it even safe to mix oxy with alcohol?"

The other girls heard me, and they all started laughing. I laughed, too, like it was a joke, but I wanted to get out of there. I wanted to get back to my room.

Several European guys had made their way over to our table and a pair of them had already latched on to a couple of the girls. One guy was trying to talk to me, but being around another man was the last thing I wanted to deal with. About a half an hour later, I was ready to go and the girls were just lit enough and occupied enough not to care. "My boyfriend makes me check in, I better get going," I said to Emily, then waved across the table to the other girls.

I was right. Nobody cared, and I was thankful to get out of there. When I got back to my room, I removed the two pills from my pocket and found the other half-pill still sitting on the bedside table. I wrapped the pills inside a Kleenex and then slipped them into a pocket in my suitcase. I didn't plan to take any more, but if I had to, I would—anything to save my career. It was all I cared about. It was the only thing that made me feel complete. I knew I was crossing a line I thought I'd never cross, but I really didn't care. And just because Amelia couldn't handle it, that didn't mean that I couldn't.

Chapter 35

THE NEXT NIGHT I had a runway that went pretty well. I didn't take any of the oxy and, though stressful, I survived it, which made me wonder if I just had gone back to work too soon. Maybe I wasn't ready.

Mae called me the next day. "What's going on? You're having trouble, and I heard you went out with Emily. Why on earth would you go out with Emily? What is going on with you, Scarlet?"

"Why do you care? I called you when I needed help and you called me a diva."

"I know I did. I'm sorry. What can I do to help you?"

"I don't know. I'm still so sad," I said, and started crying.

"Don't cry. Don't cry. You have a shoot tomorrow."

"I know, but I'm just having such a hard time. There's nothing I want more than to be working, but nobody is happy with my work anymore."

"Scarlet, honey, take it easy, okay? No pressure. You do what you need to do to get yourself back on track. I'm serious. Just take it easy and don't worry about anything. You'll get it back. I know you. Just don't do anything stupid. Rest today, maybe get a massage, get a good night's sleep. Everything will be okay. Okay?"

"Okay. Thank you." After I hung up, I called the spa and made an appointment for a massage and facial.

My cell phone rang and it was Rex. "Hi Scarlet. How are you doing? I really miss you. I can't stop thinking about you."

I didn't know what to say, so I said what he probably wanted me to say, "I've been thinking about you, too." It was the best I could do and it was true, but I was pretty sure I wasn't thinking about him the way he would have wanted. I was starting to feel angry, more at myself than Rex, but I was sad because of the way I lost my virginity. I was saving myself. I wanted it to be special, but it wasn't special; I cried, and I made Rex cry, and I bled all over my couch. It just happened so fast. I didn't know why I wasn't able to speak up and tell him to wait, but I made a huge mistake and now a part of me wanted to pull away.

"Will you be home next week?"

"Yes, unless another job comes up. I'm hoping my schedule gets busy again. But I'll let you know."

"Great. I can't wait to see you," he said.

Chapter 36

I GOT HOME a couple days early, because I had been asked to leave. The bosses on the set said they saw that I was still under a lot of stress and wanted me to take more time before coming back. They assured me that they were anxious for my return, but I knew they said that to try to make me feel better. I knew how it worked. They push the older models aside to make room for the younger models, in search of the next great girl. I could tell Mae was disappointed in me, too.

I didn't bother calling Rex. I still needed space from everyone and everything. When I picked up my dry cleaning, I noticed that there was a liquor store right next door. I put my clothes in the car, then went into the liquor store. Unsure if I'd ever been in one before, I decided I'd try wine for the first time. It's supposed to be somewhat good for you. "Where's your wine?" I asked. As I looked around, I assumed I had been in a liquor store with Amelia before, but I wasn't sure. She hadn't always been open about her drinking. And now, neither was I. I put the bottle in my bag and walked back to my car.

At home, I didn't want to talk to anybody, so I turned the ringer off on my phone and made sure my door was double bolted. I turned on the TV and started watching a movie on the Hallmark channel. It was something Amelia and I had done in the past and it was a good memory. I turned the TV toward the kitchen and poured myself a glass of wine.

From Amelia's old bedroom closet, I pulled out a small suitcase and carried it to the kitchen table. When I opened it and saw all of Amelia's beads, tools and leather for her bracelets, I felt the tears coming, so I quickly drank my glass of wine and poured another. Nothing was happening. I felt nothing. Maybe I was immune. Maybe alcohol didn't affect me the way it did Amelia. I picked through her beads and leather straps. There was a box, like a fishing tackle box, filled with wire, tools and more beads and crystals. I had no idea what I was doing. I didn't know how to make jewelry. I drank down my next glass and refilled.

After a few attempts to create a beautiful bracelet, I gave up and went back to the couch to watch another Hallmark movie. It felt great to finally relax and stop worrying about everybody. I stayed on the couch the rest of the day, napping and watching movie after movie about love and relationships with happy endings. I felt no stress and I didn't bother going to bed, I just curled up and slept like a baby all night on the same couch where Rex had taken my virginity, but I didn't even care. It barely crossed my mind.

Chapter 37

SO I DID it, big deal, I drank and took drugs. I wasn't that impressed. The wine made me tired and the oxy seemed to relax me a little, made the pain go away and made me forget about everything that had gone wrong in my life the last few months. And for that, I was thankful. I really needed a break from reality. But I decided that I wouldn't drink again or take any more oxy.

After checking my messages it was clear that maybe Rex never had intended to break up with me, or maybe because I had sex with him he decided to stick around a little longer. He had called several times. His messages were all about strengthening our relationship and rebuilding trust. He said he wanted to wait to make love, wait until we felt good together again. He kept saying he was going to make it up to me.

Make what up to me? He didn't do anything wrong. I could have screamed for him to stop and he would have, but I didn't, so I didn't know why he felt so bad. It was my fault. I never told him that I hadn't been with anybody. I had planned on telling him while we were making out, but everything happened so fast. I didn't know what to do. It wasn't that big of a deal, I'm a grown up. It was just sex. Big deal. Besides, I didn't know anybody my age who hadn't had sex yet.

There was also a message from Tabitha. "Scarlet, it's me. I hope you're doing okay. I… I was hoping I could come over this weekend to talk. I've made a terrible mistake. I'm sorry for not being there for you and for not calling you back," she said, and started crying. "I don't want to explain on your voicemail. I want to talk in person. I love you. Please call me back."

I didn't call her back. Instead, I turned my phone off again and decided to go visit Amelia. This time, on the way I stopped to buy flowers for her grave. I picked out a bouquet of snapdragons and wildflowers, bright colors mixed with some pastels—beautiful and colorful like Amelia.

I looked for the cat. I even called out to her, but she wasn't there. I placed the flowers by the front of her stone and sat in silence. While picking at the dead grass, I finally spoke to my sister. "Well, I tried OxyContin, and I drank a bottle of wine. Not at the same time." I kind of laughed. "I did it because I'm not doing so great with modeling anymore." I started crying. "I don't think I'm good at anything anymore. With you gone, I'm just a mess. I don't even know if I want to live." I stopped talking because I couldn't believe what I had just said, but it was probably true. I didn't know what I had to live for.

"Why'd you have to die? Why, Amelia? You had so much to offer. So talented, beautiful, fun, crazy… I just never thought this would happen. Not you. You were too special. I didn't think God would ever do that to you… Take you away from me… You were invincible…

"I don't know what I'm going to do. I don't care about Rex anymore. I don't think I care about modeling anymore, either."

Chapter 38

ABOUT FIFTEEN MINUTES before leaving to meet Tabitha for lunch, I took my last pill. I just wanted to be calm, and I didn't want to cry. I didn't think the talk was going to change anything, but I was at least willing to hear her out.

"Scarlet, I made one of the biggest mistakes of my life when I started ignoring you," she said as she sat down across from me.

It was worse than that, but I'll let it slide. I really don't care.

"Let me explain. As you know, I wanted to date Pete. You gave me great advice when you told me to be hard to get. That's what I did, and he started chasing me. Before I knew it, we were in a relationship. I know I neglected our friendship and I wasn't there for you when Amelia died. I'm so sorry. I was consumed by Pete, and he was pretty demanding of my time. He forced his beliefs on me and talked badly about my friends. And because you were my best friend, he was relentless when talking about you. I started to lose myself, my friends and my own common sense."

I told you he wasn't right for you. I knew the day you told me you had a fling with him, that he would be bad for you.

"Somehow I had it in my head that I would marry Pete and we would live happily ever after, a remarkable doctor team. He made me believe that he was all I needed in life. I lost a few friends because of Pete. You're lucky you weren't close enough to witness the head games he played with me... and my crazy behavior because of it."

I did witness it. I kind of laughed out loud.

Tabitha looked puzzled, but kept on talking. "If we lived closer and you had seen my behavior, I'm sure you would have set me straight, and I probably would have listened to you."

Yeah, right.

"I was listening to Pete more than I was listening to myself. I was dating an asshole who turned me against you and everybody. I jumped to his conclusions about Amelia. Scarlet, I knew your history with her. I knew how destructive she had been to you over the years. But even if you could have saved..."

Shut up! I don't care! I wanted to scream. *I don't want to hear it!*

"Scarlet, are you okay?" She leaned toward me and reached for my hand.

Oh, no, we're not doing that. I pulled my hand back.

"I'm sorry," she said and leaned back. She stared into my eyes and said, "Scarlet, you know Amelia's death wasn't your fault, right? You couldn't have done one thing to save her. You know that, right?" She waited for me to answer.

Wow. Look how quickly you change your position now that Pete dumped you. "You know, Tabitha, I really don't care. I just don't care and I don't think I want to talk about it anymore. I guess you said everything you wanted to say?"

"I want our friendship back the way it was. That's what I came here to say, and I'll do whatever I have to do to get you back. I know I hurt you and I'm sorry."

"Thanks," I said, but my tone was flat. It sounded strange, so I said it again, "Thanks." And it still sounded flat, lifeless.

"Scarlet," Tabitha started to cry. "What's wrong? You're not acting like yourself."

"What do you think is wrong? I mean, I don't know what to say. I'm not sure I feel the same about our friendship. I just don't care." I shrugged my shoulders. "I gotta go. Take care of yourself. Good luck with everything." I stood to leave.

"Scarlet, don't go."

"I have to," I said, and left the restaurant.

Chapter 39

BECAUSE I HAD taken my last pill before my talk with Tabitha, I decided to stop off at the hospital to see Dr. Windel.

"I'm doing pretty good," I told him. "I'm back to work and spending time with my boyfriend. But ever since Amelia died, I've been under a lot of stress and I'm starting to get migraines. Another model has the same problem and she gave me an oxy-cotton, I think that's how you say it." I played dumb. "Anyway, I only took half the pill, but within twenty minutes, I was able to function again. I was so thankful to her. Even though I know I shouldn't take somebody else's prescription, I was desperate, so I tried it. I was wondering if you know of anything I can take that would help me through…"

"You're right. You shouldn't take somebody else's prescription. You're also right that OxyContin can be a miracle drug for migraine sufferers. Because you've tried it and it works, I'm going to prescribe you the smallest dosage just to get you through this hard time," he said, nodding sympathetically. "I want you to check back with me in a month unless you're still having migraines. It wouldn't hurt to set you up with a doctor to have a good physical. Have you talked to a counselor?"

"Yes, I go every week," I lied.

"That's great, Scarlet. You hang in there, okay? It's great to see you again. Say hello to your mother."

"I will. Thank you, and I'll see you in a month, or sooner if I need to."

I walked out of his office and took the elevator downstairs to the pharmacy, thinking he had to be the stupidest doctor I'd ever met. It was so easy to make up a story and get a prescription for OxyContin. How could he just write out a prescription so easily without even asking me any questions or knowing anything about me?

It didn't go quite as smoothly at the pharmacy. I had to fill out a form and they had to make a copy of my driver's license. I didn't bother running it through my insurance and was surprised how expensive the prescription was. But I was happy. I left the hospital with a full bottle of oxy.

I was so excited I decided to call Rex. "Maybe we should have dinner at my place tonight."

I could tell he was excited. "Yes, Scarlet. I've missed you so much," he said.

"Great! How about seven? And I'll order pizza from your favorite place."

"You sound great, Scarlet. I can't wait to catch up. I want to hear all about your trip to Europe and everything you've been doing."

Chapter 40

I WAS PRETTY excited to see Rex but mainly because I wanted to try to be with him again. Around six I took an oxy and jumped in the shower to get ready for our date. About quarter to seven I ordered the pizza and eagerly waited for Rex.

He arrived on time and gave me his usual big hug. He looked great and smelled faintly of cologne. I just knew it was going to be a great night. The pizza came and we sat on the couch and ate, while talking and laughing and catching up on everything that had happened to each of us since that fateful night. He kept saying that I seemed so happy, and he kept asking if I was okay.

"I'm doing good, and modeling's going great. Oh, did I tell you, Tabitha called me? She wants to be friends again."

"That's great! Well that must be why you're so... I don't know... happy."

I couldn't believe how easy it was to lie and how everybody believed me. "I guess. I'm just trying to get on with my life, that's all." I leaned over and kissed him.

I lifted my plate off my lap, then took his plate from him and set them both on the coffee table. I reached for his hand, wanting him to follow me.

"What's this? Where are we going?" Saying nothing, I led the way to my bedroom. "Scarlet, come on. I don't think it's a good idea; not yet," he said, but continued to follow me. "Are you sure?"

"I'm sure," I said, and got onto the bed. He lay down next to me and gently kissed me. He was caressing me like it was my first time. He was gentle and kept asking me, while touching me, if every step forward was okay. He was amazing, and he felt amazing. It was exactly what I pictured my first time would be like.

After we finished, I couldn't stop smiling. He rolled over on his side and he smiled, too, then grabbed ahold of me and hugged me tightly. "I love you, Scarlet," he said. I didn't say anything, just stared at the ceiling and smiled. I didn't want to ruin it by talking. "Scarlet, I love you. I'm crazy in love with you and I want to spend the rest of my life with you. I know this is happening fast, but it's how I feel. I didn't know I could feel this way about anybody."

I said nothing.

"Scarlet, honey, are you okay?"

I forced myself to speak so he wouldn't panic. "Never been better."

He snuggled close to me and held me, and we both fell asleep.

When we woke up I still felt pretty good and he seemed happy, too. We warmed up the pizza and watched the news before calling it a night. After he left, I went straight back to bed, and kept thinking about how Rex said he loved me. I wanted to love him, too, but I didn't know if I did. I felt nothing. I wasn't sad or happy. I wasn't angry or upset. I wasn't excited or anxious. Sadly, I wasn't feeling love toward Rex, either, and I wasn't concerned with how he felt about me.

I felt nothing, and it was good to feel nothing.

Chapter 41

AFTER SPENDING A couple of days lying around high, watching Lifetime movies, and avoiding Tabitha and Rex as much as possible, I was bored. I crawled on the floor into my bedroom and opened my hope chest. It held nothing for my future, only keepsakes and photo albums from my past. I opened the first book and saw several pictures of Amelia and me sitting on a huge, old turtle. I started to cry. Amelia was so pretty, even at a young age, and then there was me, awkward and not happy about having my picture taken. I giggled. I didn't know how that girl in the picture became a model. The whole thing seemed like a lie, and I doubted I'd ever model again. I lifted the clear film and pulled out the picture of us on the tur-tle. I crawled back into the kitchen and stood up to hang it on my refrigerator as a reminder that I wasn't meant to be a model.

Back in my bedroom, I paged through a scrapbook of my early modeling days, but I was disgusted and slammed the book shut. I liked how it sounded—like that part of my life was over, finished. I looked through another photo album, seeing just the three of us, Mom, Amelia and me. I couldn't believe what a lie we all were, just a group of three phonies. *And I'm the biggest phony of them all.*

I was pretty sure that nobody would suspect that I was taking drugs. They would just assume I was under a lot of stress from losing my sister. But truthfully, I wasn't under much stress at all, and I was actually kind of enjoying my life for the first time. I had no responsibility, nobody to worry about, and nothing that important to do. I didn't even have to clean my townhome, and it was starting to get messy, but I didn't care.

I came across photos from one of my birthday parties at Casa Bonita, when I was probably ten or eleven. Mostly, the photos were of Tabitha, Amelia and me, with Mom taking the pictures, but there was one with all four of us. We looked happy, except for Amelia, who looked bored. I smiled, remembering that day, and then I had a brilliant idea and called Rex and said, "How about Casa Bonita for an early dinner tonight?"

He excitedly agreed. "I haven't been to that place for so long," he said.

I hadn't been there for years either. I wanted to go there because I wanted to remember my childhood, when I still had my mom, my sister and my best friend in my life. So, at five thirty when I was ready to go and Rex was running a little late, I decided to take half a pill. Rex seemed to like me more—and I liked me more—when I was a little more relaxed. I put the prescription bottle in my purse just in case I needed the other half.

At the restaurant, Rex and I got our food and were escorted to our table. "Scarlet, this place hasn't changed at all."

"I was just thinking the same thing. I can't believe it." I had so many fun memories of Casa Bonita. For several years, Tabitha and I had gone at least twice a year, once with her parents for her birthday, and once with my mom and Amelia for my birthday. And just like when I was a kid, I couldn't wait to finish eating, so I could go exploring and play games.

Rex and I watched the cliff diver and gorilla show while we ate. I think we were both taken back to our childhoods. We didn't talk much, but occasionally nodded and smiled at each other. I was starting to feel close to him again and it felt great. I had butterflies in my stomach and as much as I'd tried to deny it, I was in love with him. After everything he'd gone through with me, he had become my best friend. He always seemed to have my best interests at heart. Maybe I did have a reason to keep living and have a good life. Maybe Marge was right—I should live a life good enough for two. I could see a good life with Rex. In that moment, I was happy.

Rex raised the flag on our table to call attention to our server. "Ready for sopapillas?"

"I'm so ready," I said excitedly.

After we finished eating and wiping the honey from our sticky hands, we made our way to Black Bart's Cave and continued exploring our favorite childhood restaurant. We shared memories, held hands and laughed a lot.

I was having such a good time, the thought crossed my mind that maybe I should sneak into a bathroom and flush the rest of the pills down the toilet. I didn't want to take them anymore. I didn't want to be numb. I wanted to feel everything while I was with Rex. He deserved to have the real me. But then I wondered about modeling, and thought maybe I should hold on to them just for modeling, just until I get over this hump.

When we got back to my place, we made love, then talked a little before he had to go.

"I sure had a nice time tonight. Thank you," I said. "I love you."

"I love you, too. Thanks for the great idea for dinner. That was fun. I'll call you tomorrow. Sleep well," he said, and turned off the light. I rolled over and had started to doze off when my bedroom light was suddenly on again and Rex was standing over me.

"Scarlet," he demanded, "what is this?" He was holding my prescription of oxy.

My heart dropped. "It's nothing, Rex. I've been having headaches."

"No, you haven't!"

"Yes, I have. Dr. Windel is setting me up to get a physical." I put my hand out for the pills. "Why did you go into my purse?"

"You're lying to me."

"No, I'm not," I said, and started to cry.

"You're lying and I'm not going to do this with you. I thought you were different." He turned to leave, then turned back and tossed the pills onto the bed. "Good luck, Scarlet," Rex said, and walked out the door.

I couldn't breathe. I was shaking and crying and my chest felt tight. I looked down at the pills and opened the container. I tipped it and let one pill slide into my hand, then closed the lid. I reached next to the bed for my bottle of water, put the pill in my mouth and swallowed it. I closed my eyes and tried to relax, but I couldn't stop crying. Rage filled me and I threw my opened bottle of water toward the bedroom door; it hit the wall and water splashed everywhere. Then I threw the bottle of pills; it opened when it crashed into the dresser and pills scattered on the floor.

I didn't bother turning off the light. I just rolled over and closed my eyes.

Chapter 42

OVER THE NEXT week I kept my phone off. I didn't eat or sleep or take care of myself. Some days, just taking a shower seemed like a huge success. I sat and stared a lot. When I couldn't stop my mind from replaying everything in my life, especially every mistake I'd ever made, every regret, every failure—that's when I'd make my way to the bedroom and take a pill off the floor.

Then, I'd start feeling a little better, and I'd start making plans for my future. *Ha, my future.* I missed my Gucci shoot in Miami, and I knew I'd never get another chance at that. I kept trying to make bracelets but they looked stupid, cheap. I didn't know what I was doing, so I had the idea to go back to Amelia's grave and get my bracelet to use as a template.

High, I drove to the cemetery. I sat down next to Amelia and started crying. "Well, I've lost Rex now, too." I laughed a little. "So let's see, let's add it up. I lost you, then Tabitha, then Mom, but she never really liked me anyway. And now Rex doesn't want me either. So that's four people who've left me in just a few months. Oh, and I'm sure Mae is finished with me, too. Modeling's done."

I heard something and turned to look. It was the cat meowing and trotting toward me. That made me cry even harder. "You're the only one left." I was so happy to see her. I leaned toward the ground so she could head-butt my face and head, and she did, and I laughed. I kept petting her, listening to her loving purr. She made me feel a little better.

I took my key and started moving the dirt around. Panicking that the bracelet was gone, I started using my fingers, but then I felt the leather and pulled it out of the dirt. It was dirty, but I was glad to have it back. I slipped it into my pocket and lay down next to Amelia. The cat crawled right up on my chest and meowed. She got comfortable and lay down. I petted her as she purred, and I drifted off to sleep.

I woke up, startled to find the cat was gone and my mother was standing over me.

"Scarlet, I've been trying to call you. We need to talk. I didn't expect to find you here, but I'm glad I did. Tabitha has been trying to get ahold of you, too."

Why can't everybody just leave me alone? I sat up and moved to the side of Amelia's grave but said nothing.

"I'm sorry I was so mean to you that day you were at my place. I didn't mean the things I said." She sat down on the other side of Amelia's grave. "I have been getting counseling," she said, and started crying. "I've made so many mistakes."

I pulled at the dried grass, but still said nothing.

"I've always had pills around, you know that. Mainly valium and sleeping pills. Amelia had barely started high school when she started telling me that she couldn't concentrate in school and some boy was stressing her out and she couldn't sleep. So one evening, I gave her half of a valium. I thought this would help her relax so she could sleep. I thought it was just a one-time thing. But then two weeks later, she needed another one because she had a big test and she wanted a good night's rest, so I gave her half a sleeping pill. She always wanted more. I didn't see the problem. I didn't think it was a big deal. I take them whenever I need them, I figured she was going to end up like me with some anxiety easily fixed by a little valium or help with a good night's sleep." She crossed her legs. "I'm probably the one who started her addiction. I'm the one who should have had a kidney for her. I'm the one who should have died. You have no idea the guilt I've lived with all these years. I gave her a valium—I gave my young daughter drugs."

I had no idea that had been going on, so I kept listening.

"Even when I knew Amelia had a problem, I couldn't admit it. I was so scared of the truth. I was scared that she would tell people that I gave her drugs when she was fifteen years old. I didn't want to be blamed. I didn't want people to think I was a bad mother. I loved you girls more than anything in the world. You were all I had. I was afraid that if Amelia got help, she would start telling the truth about me. I would be the one who ruined her life. I was the adult; I should have known better. I was her first drug pusher. I never wanted to face it, and I never wanted to hear it said out loud. But it was ringing in my head every day. So loud, so loud."

I don't care, and it doesn't change anything.

"After Amelia died, I still wanted to find somebody to blame, so I blamed you. I'm so sorry for that. I should have been there for you. I should have been strong for you."

"Whatever," I finally said.

"Scarlet, Amelia was so sick nobody could have saved her. If we had gotten to her sooner, like a year ago, we might have had a chance. But Amelia didn't want to quit drinking. Even from the hospital bed with a tube in her arm for dialysis, she asked me to go buy her some vodka."

"Did you?" I snapped.

"No, but I almost did." She exhaled loudly. "She begged me, she cried, pleaded, but I didn't. I knew somebody would and I was right. A couple guys brought her stuff while she was in the hospital. I knew, and the doctors knew. We tried to put restrictions on visitors, but they still found their way in. Amelia didn't want to stop drinking. She wouldn't have stopped. That's why I prevented you from doing the surgery. I knew it would kill you if she kept drinking and drugging on your kidney. I didn't care about my kidney, but I was pretty sure the doctors wouldn't have let anybody donate to her. She was too sick physically and emotionally. There wasn't much hope. My counselor is helping me see that now."

"I don't know what you want me to say. Congratulations? I'm so sorry? You're the greatest mom in the world?" I stood up to leave. "I have to go."

"I just wanted you to hear me out. I lost Amelia and I don't want to lose you, too."

That's not what you said last time we talked. I'm pretty sure you told me you wish I died instead of Amelia. That's what I heard.

"I'm working through my guilt and some of my issues. Maybe you should talk to a counselor, too, and work through some of yours."

Fuck off! Leave me alone! I turned to leave.

"Please don't go," she said, and stood up.

I turned back and held up my hand to make it clear I didn't want her to follow me. Then I walked to my car. None of that even mattered to me. I didn't give a shit about any of it. I was high on oxy. Maybe I couldn't have saved her, maybe I could have. *Who cares? She's dead. Does it really even matter?*

Chapter 43

WHEN I GOT back to my place, Tabitha was sitting at my door. "Fantastic," I said sarcastically. If she hadn't seen me, I would have turned and walked the other way. I wasn't in the mood for any more of this. I just wanted to lock myself in my place and be left alone. I wanted to lie on the couch and watch movies.

"Rex called me and told me that you're taking OxyContin."

"None of your business and I don't want to talk to you." I stepped by her to open my door. "You're not coming in."

"Oh, yes, I am," she said, and got to her feet quickly. "In fact, I'm not leaving you until you're back to yourself. I took a leave from work and I'm staying with you. My suitcase is in the car."

I shook my head and tried to get inside the door without her, but she easily pushed her way in. She grabbed the keys from me and said, "You're not doing this. I won't let you." She fought back tears. "You're my best friend, and I'm not going to let you destroy yourself."

I tried to fight back my tears. I didn't want to cry, but I felt defeated. "I don't know what I'm doing."

"I know."

"I don't want you here," I said.

"I know."

"Why can't you just leave me alone? You have to leave." I reached for my phone. "I'll call the police."

"Good. Call 'em," she said.

"What is wrong with you? Get out of my house!"

"I'm not leaving."

"I wish you would mind your own business." I threw my coat on the couch. "Why can't you mind your own business?"

"You are my business, Scarlet. Speaking of business, I called Mae and she's on her way here, too."

I went to the couch to sit down. "I just need some time to myself. Why can't you understand that? I'm sad right now, and I don't want to be around people."

"Rex is coming over, too," she said. "Scarlet, I know you're in pain. We want to be with you to help you work through it. None of us realized how hard this would be on you. You put on a good front. We understand now, and we're not leaving you. We're not giving up on you."

"Didn't you just hear me? I want to be alone!" I felt the bracelet in my pocket and started to cry. "Why can't everybody just leave me alone? What is wrong with everyone?"

Chapter 44

MY INTERVENTION LASTED a solid five days. Mae, Rex, and even Dr. Pape and Marge took turns with me, while Tabitha stayed with me the entire time. She cooked for me, sat in the bathroom with me while I showered, slept in my bed with me. She even sat outside the bathroom door when I had to go to the bathroom, sometimes making me laugh. She never left my side.

They didn't make me talk at all. They just stayed with me, often holding my hand. I cried a lot. Sometimes they cried with me. And for the first time in a long time, I didn't feel alone. I started to feel loved. I started to believe I wasn't the horrible person I thought I was. There was no other explanation: why else would these people stay by my side like they did, even when I tried so desperately to make them go away, if they didn't love me?

I decided to go into treatment after spending the five days with those who loved me. Because of the short time I was using oxy, I didn't have to go through any type of detox. But I had to get my life back to the way it was, and I never wanted to drink or take drugs again.

I couldn't really say that I was a full-on addict, but I was willingly headed in that direction. I skipped the partying and fun part of addiction and went straight to using drugs and alcohol to numb my pain. I didn't want to feel anything. Every thought, every memory, all the guilt, hurt too much. I took oxy just to survive another day. The more I did it, the more I hated myself, because I knew what I was doing was wrong. I didn't care because at times I wasn't even sure I wanted to live. I knew I had the disease in me. My dad had it. My sister had it. And maybe my mom had some form of it, too.

I thought treatment would give me a better understanding of Amelia. I wanted to connect with people like her, but mostly, I wanted a better connection with myself. I needed answers to why all of this happened.

I wasn't running away from anything or anyone. Instead, I was trying to get closer to people. It was new for me, and it was not easy opening up to strangers, but through the group meetings and counseling sessions I was learning to forgive myself for not being perfect. I wasn't the perfect sister, daughter, or friend and that was okay.

During my counseling sessions with Dr. Smart, which was a perfect name for her because she was brilliant, I learned that I was focusing too much on loss. "I hear a running theme with you, Scarlet—loss. It seems your whole thought process is dependent on what you might lose or what you have already lost. I believe you're motivated by fear of loss, instead of getting excited about all you have in your life and everything you have to gain from living your truth. It's possible you're making poor decisions in order to evade loss and that isn't living in freedom. It's as if your fears have caged you in."

I was intrigued and listened carefully as I took notes in my journal. I could relate to what she was saying, because it was true.

"I'd like to see you get excited about your bright future," Dr. Smart said. "Loss happens to everybody; it's what makes life interesting and crazy and scary and fun, and yes, sad, too. Loss is what builds our character and teaches us how strong we are. And we have a choice, we can either let loss destroy us or we can embrace it and stop living in fear. It all comes down to a choice, Scarlet."

"Losing my sister was not fun or interesting. It's the worst thing I've ever gone through and I'm still suffering," I said.

"I know, and I'm not discounting what you've been through. My heart breaks for you," she said, putting both her hands on her heart. "I want you focusing on the good in your life. Tonight, I'd like you to write in your journal about everything you have that's good, especially what you fear losing." She smiled and said, "I know it can be terrifying, but trust me, there is method to my madness."

That night I tried to remember everything Dr. Smart and I talked about. I started by writing down what I was grateful for and what I didn't want to lose. Modeling was first on my list because it was my passion and my financial security. Tabitha was next, and then Rex. Then my list continued with things that were important, but not strongly connected to me. Sadly, I felt indifference toward my mom because it felt like I had already lost her a long time ago. Again, my thoughts drifted to everything I had lost: Amelia, recent jobs, and even my virginity. Dr. Smart was right. My mind kept going back to loss and fear and sadness, but also disappointment with myself. I didn't want to be so down and negative; I wanted to be optimistic and positive.

I didn't sleep much that night, because I kept thinking about my life, especially the last few months. I was somehow living a self-fulfilling prophecy. Everything I feared, I created. In the last few months, I had lost everything I was holding on to so tightly. I tried to keep my family together. I wanted to save Amelia but I lost her anyway. I temporarily lost Tabitha and Rex, and I wasn't even sure they'd be there when I finished with treatment. I was not sure about my career, either. And yet, I was still alive and still had a future. I took a deep breath. *Why do I do this to myself?*

After a restless night, I went to my group's yoga class that morning. I dreaded it because yoga reminded me of Amelia and I didn't want to be sad anymore. The first fifteen minutes of yoga was meditation time, so I closed my eyes and tried to clear my mind. But all I could think about was Amelia and the big secret we shared.

~~~~

I came home to find that Amelia had moved back in with me. And she had brought a white cat with her that she adopted from a shelter. "I know I didn't ask you, but I'll take care of her. Totally my responsibility," she said, pleading for my approval.

I gave in. "Just so we're on the same page—I'm fine with you having a cat, but you know I can't take care of her," I said as I reached for the white furry critter. "What's her name?"

"Mystic."

"I like it. How'd you come up with that name?" I asked, as Mystic rubbed her face against mine.

"I wanted to name her Unicorn, like my tattoo, but it didn't sound right, so I went with Mystic. It fits her. She's magical, healing, beautiful, and free from that terrible shelter." She leaned in and kissed Mystic on the head.

Remembering my unicorn, I felt a twinge of unease, but I ignored it, and said, "She's purring. I love her."

"Me, too," Amelia said. "She's a year old."

"Ah, she's just a kitten." I snuggled my face in closer as she purred. "House trained?" I asked, closing one eye and hoping the answer was yes.

"Of course. Her box is in my room, so you have to stop closing my bedroom door."

"Then keep your room clean," I said.

"Done." She took my hand and led me to her bedroom.

The blinds were open and the light was streaming in. Her room was clean. "Oh, my God. What happened?"

"Ha, ha," she said sarcastically. "I even returned most of your clothes."

"In my dry cleaning bag?" I said, figuring she wanted me to get them cleaned so she could take them again.

"No, hanging in your closet." She punched me gently in the arm. "I had them cleaned. And I'll ask from now on. It's just that you have so many great designer clothes."

I didn't know how she had done it, but I could tell she was clean and sober. Pregnancy might be the magic that saved my sister. For the first time, she thought more about others, and about me. I put Mystic down and she rubbed up against my leg, then trotted to Amelia and rubbed up against her leg, too. We both laughed, then headed back to the living room, with Mystic following close behind. I sat on the couch and Amelia plopped down right next to me, almost sitting on my lap. Then Mystic jumped up with us.

This was the sister I wanted to hold on to.

Amelia was nesting. She was cleaning, straightening the house, and caring for Mystic and maybe for me, too. "How are you doing?" I asked.

"I'm great. Just over eleven weeks. I don't know how they can figure that out, but that's what they think," she said.

"When will we know if it's a boy or a girl? And when will you start to show?"

"I already show." She put my hand on her belly and we both laughed.

I couldn't tell, but I pretended I could. "I think I felt a kick."

"I know it's a girl," she said with her hand resting on mine. "I want a girl just like you."

~~~~

In the middle of the yoga class, I fell over on my side, sobbing. I couldn't stop crying and moaning through the pain. I curled up in the fetal position and some of the girls from the group sat around me, each placing a hand on my back to let me know that they were there. I wasn't alone. "I thought I had more time with her," I wailed. "I never thought I would lose her."

When I finally got my emotions under control, I was excused from class to write in my journal. I grabbed a jacket and my journal and went outside.

While Amelia was pregnant, she found a DVD and started doing prenatal yoga. It was her first time, and as I had never done yoga, either, I sometimes joined her. But usually we laughed more than we exercised, because Mystic wouldn't leave us alone.

After Amelia's miscarriage, she moved out and left Mystic with me. I wanted so badly to keep her, but I knew I couldn't take care of her. I paid a fair amount of money to the shelter to help keep her alive and help them find her a good home. Mystic deserved a good home, a good family.

I cried as I wrote about more losses. When Amelia lost her baby, I lost Amelia again, I lost my niece, and I lost Mystic.

Chapter 45

AFTER MANY GROUP discussions, yoga classes, A.A. meetings, and time with Dr. Smart, I felt better than I ever had. All the hard work had led me to understand that I was never capable of saving Amelia from her problems. I had to let go of the heartache and guilt I felt toward her and myself, so I could focus on the good memories I had with Amelia. I loved remembering her bracelets, and Mystic, and the times we laughed together, and the times she tried to get her life back. I remembered the times she was good to me, when she *was* my big sister. In some ways I felt closer to her now than I did when she was alive. And that had always been my goal, to be closer to her.

When I was released from treatment, Rex was there to pick me up. His big smile told me he was proud of me, and I immediately felt a sense of security. He handed me a bouquet of red roses, gave me a big hug, then got down on one knee and said, "Scarlet, I want to spend my life loving you. Will you marry me?"

"Yes!" I said, and leaned down to kiss him.

He slipped the sparkling diamond ring on my finger. "No pressure to set a date. We'll get to that. I just want you to know that I'm here, and I'll always be here for you."

We got into his pickup, and I scooted in close to him. As we drove home, he told me that Tabitha would be staying with me next weekend to catch up. "Now, Mae is busy with new clients, but she has booked several jobs for you in the next couple weeks," he said, and looked at me. "Are you up for it?"

I was so happy, I wanted to cry, but I was also scared. I kept looking at my new ring and realized I was no longer protected by the treatment center and my support system. I was nervous, but excited, too. "Rex, I'm a little shaky."

"I remember that feeling," he said, and smiled. "You're going to be okay." He gave my leg a gentle squeeze. "I sure missed you."

"I missed you, too. I love you."

~~~~

After only a few weeks, I had my life back better than it was before and I was grateful for everybody who helped me. I never had a lot of friends or a lot of people around me for support, but I realized that having a couple of lifelong soul mates was better than having countless friends who come and go. I was blessed to have Tabitha, Mae, and Rex. They loved me in my darkest moments. They put me first in their lives when I needed them.

Mae really came through for me and helped save my career. I'd been steadily booked over the last couple of weeks, with a trip to Dubai on my calendar next week. I was edgy about that trip, but ready to face my career head on.

Rex was my biggest support. He was my security and my strength. He was that safe place when I needed one.

But it was Tabitha who saved my life. She was the one who rallied the troops for me, and she refused to let me end up like Amelia, when it seemed so many wanted to walk away.

~~~~

As for Amelia, I needed to keep her close to me and I needed to do something in honor of her. So, because I was not gifted at making jewelry, I hired a talented young woman to copy the bracelets that Amelia had made, and started a little side jewelry business called *Amelia's Gifts*. A portion of the proceeds goes to a local women's recovery center in Amelia's name. Dr. Pape actually started the program to help women struggling with addiction in honor of *her* sister. I hoped Amelia was proud of what she inspired.

Amelia had a lot of gifts. She was a beautiful, talented, intelligent woman who deserved a better life.

I'm going to try my hardest to live a life good enough for two, for both of us.

Visit L.E. Get at

https://authorleget.wordpress.com/
https://www.twitter.com/LE_Get